# BO-MÈ

## (The Ladies)

# BO-MÈ

## (The Ladies)

### Cecile Stratton

Order this book online at www.trafford.com
or email orders@trafford.com

Most Trafford titles are also available at major online book retailers.

© Copyright 2010, 2011 Cecile Stratton.

All rights reserved. No part of this publication may be reproduced, stored in a retrieval system, or transmitted, in any form or by any means, electronic, mechanical, photocopying, recording, or otherwise, without the written prior permission of the author.

Printed in the United States of America.

ISBN: 978-1-4269-5348-4 (sc)

*Trafford rev. 02/17/2011*

 www.trafford.com

North America & International
toll free: 1 888 232 4444 (USA & Canada)
phone: 250 383 6864 ♦ fax: 812 355 4082

When you are born, your work is placed
in your heart.
— Kahlil Gibran

Did you know that Canada and Africa
danced to the same (geological) beat?
— David Suzuki

["The Great Lakes, a Geological Journey"]

For my late husband John
and all those who, with me believed in my dream over the years
and the Basuto so dear to me. It was
a long gestation period, but gratifying!

# PREFACE

This is not an autobiography, although some of the story is built around the experiences of the author who taught in Lesotho, Zambia and Nigeria.

The early sixties was the time when the various mission churches wielded a strong influence, especially in nursing and education. International governments, to pacify their political world conscience, set up agencies to send help. These workers laboured under the aegis of the various denominations established there.

Racism in South Africa had an entirely different meaning back then—it related only to relations between the South Africans of British stock and those of Dutch origin. Blacks were a "native problem". They were considered sub-human; just "kaffirs" or pagans.

Some readers may wish to identify with certain places, people or events. If this occurs, then the author will have accomplished the task of criss-crossing between the real and the fictitious with skill.

Fact and fiction are woven into a story, in an attempt to share with the reader the very full and rich life of the author. Welcome to my world!

October, 2010, Windsor, Ontario<br>
Cecile Stratton

# PART ONE
## Johnna

> Johnna Rymhs, the main character, is a Canadian nun from Souris, Manitoba. She is sent to teach in Basutoland, South Africa in the early sixties. She maintains a close bond with three of her students over thirty-five years

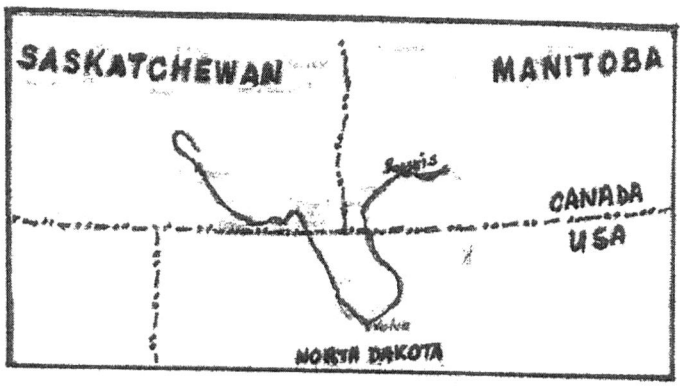

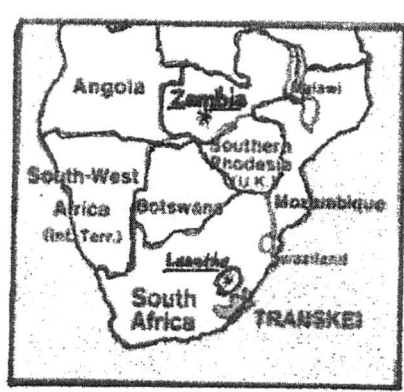

# Chapter One

John Rymhs stood on the roof of his storage shed, which had been built into the side of the hill by his grandfather at the turn of the century. The family had immigrated from Bukovinia, a region divided by Romania and the Ukraine in southeastern Europe's Carpathian Mountains. In 1896, Canada initiated its first major immigration by soliciting new settlers from Eastern Europe. Over the years, 170,000 Ukrainian peasants had come to escape economic and national oppression by the Russians. At first they had settled in Ontario but moved to the Prairies when these provinces opened up to homesteading. Federal government surveyors divided the land into townships consisting of 36 sections per mile square. The CPR and the Hudson Bay Company claimed parcels of land, while the rest was opened for homesteading. Any male eighteen years of age or older could apply for a quarter section; the cost was ten dollars. The duties of the homesteader were to live on the land at least six months a year for three years and break a number of acres of prairie sod.

The small poplars that grew along the bluffs of the river were free for the taking and the settlers used them as roof supports, in the caves of their storage sheds. John's family shed had been renewed many times over the years. When they were wheat farmers, they stored the wheat for drying but now that John was a horse rancher, he stored his hay there. He came here whenever he had decisions to make or just for peace and quiet. Today he had invited his second son, Marco to meet him. As they looked southward over the Souris River Valley, John said;

"Follow the Souris River as far as your eye can see, son. If you were a bird, you could follow the 720 km river to its source. From here you'd fly south to North Dakota, then on to Velva where you would turn north again towards Saskatchewan. Across the Canadian border, you would go past Estevan, to the Yellow Grass Marshes north of Weyburn where the river rises. All along the way you'd see "blocks" of Ukrainian settlements."

"If the settlements along the river are Ukrainian, why is the river called by a French name like souris?"

"Prior to 1881," his father said, "it was called Plum Creek. The French had set up seven fur-trade posts along its banks. At a certain vantage point, the river looked like mouse tracks. That is why the French called it souris which is the French for mouse."

"Surely, Dad, you haven't called me up here to talk about the river?"

"No, but you should know your origins and be proud of them. Of course many other nationalities settled here, but it was the Ukrainians who stuck to farming. It was a very hard life but they stuck to it, like the gumbo in the spring. A family had to clear the land before they could build their houses, barns and storage sheds. They used bullocks and horses to remove the stumps. They raised cattle, pigs, and chickens and fished all year to satisfy their protein requirements. Of course everyone had a family garden. The grain crops were not dependable; they were vulnerable to the weather. I kept buying up the quarter sections from the poor buggers that couldn't make a go of it. When I had enough land for my family, I started to upgrade my homestead. That's why I called you up here today."

"I still don't understand why up here of all places."

"Look to the east. See the land between our place and that of old man Forrest's semi-precious stones mine and quarry? It is my gift to you, for your upcoming wedding to that lovely Kathleen O'Leary. It's your very own quarter section, son. After the harvest, both families will help put up the buildings to get you started on your own. O'Leary has said that he would supply all the necessary materials from his shop at no interest to be paid back when you can. On your twenty-first birthday, I gave you five horses. Now you can start your own ranch sooner. That's why I met you up here today."

Marco's voice was full of emotion as he whispered, "Thanks, Dad!"

"Just make that beautiful lady of yours happy and that will be all the thanks I need."

Marco left his father on the roof and literally flew home. He corralled his horse and hitched Old Bessie to the cabriolet and was off in a cloud of dust. His mother, watching from the window, thought he had gone plum loco. He burst into the general store and greeted Mr. O'Leary.

"May I see Kitty?"

"Blarney! It must be mighty important to come barging in here so early in the day!"

"Oh, it is, Mr. O'Leary, it is!"

Kitty heard all the commotion from her office at the back of the store and came out when she recognized Marco's voice.

"Why Marco, is someone ill?"

"No, Kit. I have a surprise to show you. Will you come with me?"

Kitty looked pleadingly at her father for permission to leave work. Mr. O'Leary thought that since he had promised to raise all the children Catholic, he could be trusted.

"Alright me dear. I'll keep an eye out here while you are gone."

The buggy sped past rows of houses in the village and stopped just beyond old man Forrest's mining enterprises. Marco pointed to an overgrown field and beamed.

"My God. Is this the surprise? A fallow field?"

"Yes it's fallow, but it is OURS! Our very own quarter section! Dad gave it to us as a wedding present! Your father has promised to supply us with the needed building materials interest-free. We can pay him back a little at a time."

"Oh Marco, how splendid! I had visions of us starting our married life living with the O'Leary clan!"

"We may have to stay with them until after the harvest, when both families will get together to build our house and barn. That shouldn't take more than two weeks at best,"

The wedding was simple. St. Patrick's Church had never seen so many Ukrainian Orthodox Catholics! The Ukrainians were too scattered on their huge farms to have a common church. They preferred to practice their Christianity at home, only attending baptisms, weddings, and burials of friends and neighbours. Kitty on the other hand was from a very pious Catholic home and had inherited a very staunch Catholic faith. Marco, not a religious man himself, admired that in her and allowed her to put pictures of Jesus and Mary in the living room. He tolerated a shrine to the Virgin for the month of May. Every

Sunday she attended church by herself and the parish priest badgered her after Mass on Sunday.

"You've been married for over a year now Kathleen, why are you not pregnant yet?"

Kitty would answer coolly but firmly, "It isn't for lack of trying, Father!"

Her forthright answer always shut him up. She never told Marco because she knew that he would criticize the priest and they had been taught never to question or criticize a priest. She could hear him saying, "What the hell business is it of his?" So she just kept quiet about it and endured in silence.

In the second year of their marriage, when they were expecting their first child, they often discussed names. Marco never complained about all the saints' names that Kitty came up with, but he was really hurt when she insisted that their first child should be called Matthew.

"Why Matthew, Kitty, there's no one in either family by that name for generations back?"

"Marco, I want to name the boys after the four Evangelists."

"You mean we are only going to have four children? What happens if we get a girl? Why not use apostles' names? That way we could have twelve," Marco said hopefully.

Two years later, when their second son was born, Marco was happy to go back to the Evangelists. They called him Mark. He couldn't argue either when two years later along came Luke. This woman really has pull with God, he thought.

Matthew was six, Mark was four and Luke was two, when on April 13$^{th}$,1933, the fourth Evangelist was born.

Marco wondered how Kitty would handle the fact that it was a girl. She was not thwarted in the least.

"We'll call her John-na," she said smilingly.

Marco watched as she sat on her bed, holding the new baby and surrounded by the boys. As he listened he marveled at the depths of her knowledge especially of all things Catholic. He realized that the boys were far too young to grasp the references and much less retain them. But on she went, knowing that repetition was the mother of education as she always said.

"From 1558 until 1829, Roman Catholics in England were not permitted to practice their faith openly and were forbidden to teach catechism, which was a set of rules of their Christian religion. Matthew has a catechism which they study at school. During that time people wrote songs and carols for young Catholics with words that had secret meanings that they explained to the children."

She sang the "The Twelve Days of Christmas" for them. When she had finished, she asked them,

"What in the world do "leaping Lords, French hens, swimming swans, and especially a partridge in a pear tree have to do with Christmas? It has two messages; the surface meaning plus a hidden meaning known only to the members of their church, which their children could learn. Each element or part of the song had a "code" word standing for a religious reality. For example, the "partridge" in a pear tree was Jesus Christ. "Two turtles doves" was the Old and New Testaments. "Three French hens" stood for faith, hope and love. "The four calling birds" were the four evangelists, Matthew, Mark, Luke and John. "The five golden rings" recalled the first five books of the Old Testament which was the "Law" given to God's people. "The six geese a'laying" stood for the six days of creation when God created the world. "The seven swans a'swimming" represents the seven gifts of the Holy Spirit, prophesy, serving, teaching, exhorting, contributing, leadership, and mercy. "The eight maids a'milking" were the eight beatitudes or blessings. "Nine ladies dancing" were the nine fruits of the Holy Spirit; love, joy, peace, patience, kindness, goodness, faithfulness, gentleness, and self-control "Ten lords-a-leaping" were the Ten Commandments. "Eleven pipers piping", were the eleven faithful apostles. "The twelve drummers drumming", were the twelve points of belief in the Apostles' Creed. Now you all know the history of one carol, but Mommy wants to sing you one about our family."

She began in her sure, sweet voice and when she had finished the first line, the boys chirped in:

"Mat-thew, Mark, Luke and John-na; bless this bed that we lie on;

Mat-thew, Mark, Luke and John-na; bless this bed that we lie on."

"You see, my darlings, that was then and this is now!"

"Mat-thew, Mark, Luke and John-na; bless this bed that we lie on;

Mat-thew, Mark, Luke and John-na; bless this bed that we lie on."

Marco was amazed. Kitty had her four Evangelists!

# Chapter Two

Saint Patrick's Church in Souris, Manitoba was like an "International Florali", with all the various spring flowers. Today, the fourth Rymhs' evangelist was being baptized! Leave it to Kitty to choose a big church festival like Pentecost, thought Marco. He wondered what Father O'Donnell's reaction would be to her choice of the name! Father could hardly say that it wasn't Christian!

"I baptize you. . . ," Father hesitated, as he read the name. "I baptize you JOHN-na," he said as he poured too much water distractedly over the child. He continued, "In the name of the Father and of the Son and of the Holy Ghost."

He knew better than to argue with Kathleen O'Leary Rymhs! I'll speak to her later he thought. Later, at the reception in the parish hall, he finally had a go at her.

"This child is going to be a great source of trouble to you with a handle like that!" he exploded.

"Father, do you remember what Simeon said about Jesus when He was presented in the temple? "This child is destined as a sign to be rejected." He certainly wasn't a lot of trouble to His mother!"

Confound that woman! How dare she compare her child to Jesus and a girl at that!

Father persisted, "Yes, but Simeon also told Mary that a sword would pierce her own heart because of that child."

Marco noticed Father O'Donnell storm away. He could tell that Kitty was upset also. When he asked her later about the incident, she said that it was nothing. She had been taught never to criticize a priest no matter how much it hurt her.

From the time Johnna was able to walk, she went everywhere with her dad. She was with him on his horse as he rounded up the herd and she helped him feed them. In winter, she went with him into the woods to chop firewood. They fished together all year. In summer it was from Canada's longest suspension bridge over the Souris River. In winter, Marco set up a small cabin on the frozen river. A kerosene stove with a chimney kept the chocolate and coffee hot. Along both sides of the cabin ran benches. In the center was a dark gaping hole from which they fished.

When Kitty complained that he spoiled Johnna rotten one day, he blewup.

"Kitty, I have let you have your way about everything. I have never contradicted you. But this time, I am going to have my own way. I want Johnna to learn how to be a real Ukrainian farmer's wife some day."

"But I am a good Ukrainian farmer's wife and I never learned all those things." she wailed.

"You are a good Ukrainian rancher's wife, not a Ukranian farmer's wife. Chances of Johnna finding a "rancher" are very slim. But there are plenty of Ukrainian farmers about."

Kitty knew that she had always had her way and Marco had never said "no" to her. She decided to let it be. She taught Johnna how to read and write, however. She read to her every day; she taught her small household chores. Johnna was a quick learner and she was very, very curious about everything. "Just like her mother!" Father O'Donnell would say, thought Kitty smiling.

One day Marco had business in Brandon, so he left at sunrise. When Johnna got up she was devastated that her father should have left without her. While her mother was busy about the house, she took her fishing rod, found some worms and was off to the river with their big German shepherd, Trixie at her heels. She never caught anything because she had improperly hooked the worms and the fish just slipped off. By early afternoon, she was hungry and decided to head for home the short way through the tall grass. She took a wrong turn and found herself at old man Dupuis' fence. She started to climb the six-foot fence but got hooked on a loose wire. Trixie tried to unhook her but to no avail. The dog knew better than to fetch the old man, who always shot at her whenever he could, so she ran home. She arrived at the ranch just as Marco was returning. He was mystified by her strange, incessant barking. Once inside the house he found Kitty in a terrible state.

"Oh, Marco! I haven't seen Johnna since after breakfast and I have searched everywhere!"

"It's ok dear. I think I know where to find her."

He followed Trixie, who kept turning around to make sure Marco was following. He found Johnna hanging on the fence like a rag doll. When she saw Marco, she began to cry at the top of her lungs. On the way home he made her promise that she would never leave home alone again.

"Daddy," she whined, "will you also promise never to leave home without me again!"

A few weeks later another incident occurred involving Johnna that frightened the Rymhs' family. The two older boys had gone off to school. Luke and Johnna were playing in the backyard. Kitty watched them from the kitchen window. She heard Johnna say to Luke that she could hide somewhere and he would never find her.

"No you can't. I know all the hideouts on the ranch," boasted Luke.

Kitty laughed at the two of them and went about her tasks only to be interrupted an hour later by Luke's crying.

"Mommy, Mommy! I have looked everywhere for Johnna and I can't find her!"

"Let's look together", she said, hiding her apprehension.

Kitty began calling Johnna's name loudly. They checked all the buildings then went into the house and made a thorough search there. Outside once more, Kitty thought she heard a cry. She followed the sound until it became louder and louder. When she reached the well, she said,

"Oh my God, Luke! Run and get Daddy and tell him to bring a ladder because Johnna has fallen into the well!"

Kitty ran into the house and picked up a flashlight, a blanket and the first aid kit. When she returned to the well, Marco had already descended into the dark pit. Johnna was covered in mud and sobbing uncontrollably when Marco brought her to the surface. They checked for broken bones and then wrapped her in the blanket. Once inside, Marco placed her gently on the kitchen table. Kitty stripped her ever so carefully and washed her through tears of gratitude. Marco held her while Kitty went to fetch her clean clothes. Soon she was as perky as ever and asked for cookies and milk. Luke remarked that she was well again! Marco went out and covered the old well that he had neglected to do for so long. He cursed himself for having jeopardized the safety of his little princess by his laziness and neglect.

Johnna was five years old when she came home one day and told Kitty and Marco that she had a job and would be needing a lunch in the morning. Her parents stiffled their laughs and Marco asked seriously,

"Where are you going to work?"

"I'm working for Mr. Brazzo next door. He said he would pay me a dollar if I would pick his carrots by Friday. He wants to sell them at the market on Saturday."

Kitty and Marco could hardly refrain from laughing at the new labourer. Mr. Brazzo lived with his widowed mother next door. He was now too old to farm but had a sizeable vegetable garden. He went every Saturday to the Souris market to sell his produce.

In the morning, after the boys had left for school, Johnna picked up the lunch box that Kitty had packed, "just like the boys" and trotted off to her new job. Around four o'clock, she traipsed in with her empty lunch box and a big sigh of fatigue.

"Did you get paid today?" Marco asked.

"No, Daddy. I've got three more rows of carrots to pick tomorrow, then Mr. Brazzo said that he would pay me."

On Saturday morning, a very angry Mr. Brazzo arrived at the Rymh's home and with a loud knock entered the kitchen shouting,

"Where is that girl?"

"Why, Mr. Brazzo? What has she done?" asked Kitty.

"Well, this morning, I looked for the carrots to take to market and couldn't find them. Where did she put them?"

Just then Johnna appeared in the kitchen.

Kitty asked, "Darling, where did you put Mr. Brazzo's carrots. He wants to bring them to the market and he can't find them?"

"Mommy, Mr. Brazzo promised that he would pay me one dollar for pulling out all the carrots. But when I finished he only gave me a quarter. So I planted all the carrots back again and left his quarter nearby"

"I'm afraid that when you promise to pay Johnna a dollar, you must pay her a dollar. She knows her money and she is a very shrewd business lady, Mr. Brazzo."

Mr Brazzo stormed out of the kitchen muttering, "Crazy Mother; crazy daughter!"

# Chapter Three

September 3, 1939, Britain and France declared war against Germany and Johnna started school. These two events would greatly change Marco's life. He wiped a tear from his eyes as he watched her trudge off with her lunch box. He knew that he had lost his faithful little companion. Later, he would see his eldest son go off to war. It seemed to have all happened so suddenly!

For Johnna school was a breeze. Her mother had taught her to read and write, so she always finished her work before the others. This gave her plenty of time for her favourite hobby—drawing. In the second week of school, she drew a scene of a wigwam and a small boy in a bathtub. On the bottom she had printed, "Luke Warmwater". At recess she gave it to Luke in the schoolyard. He was always playing "Cowboys and Indians" and he just hated to take a bath. His friends had all gathered around and to his embarrassment, began to tease him. He chased Johnna, swearing to get even with her.

As time went on, Johnna still showed very shrewd business sense. She thought that she was teasing rather than stealing, as she took Matthew's large "Indian Head" pennies, one by one. She sold them at school for five cents. Then she would run over to her granddad O'Leary's store and buy candy. This was fun and it went on for months until the pennies were all finished and Matthew noticed that they had disappeared. It didn't take long to learn who the culprit was and Marco knew that he would have to take Johnna to the back shed for a strapping. When he saw her there so small and fragile, he didn't have the heart to strap her.

"Darling, you must never take anything that belongs to someone else. That's called stealing. Promise me that you will never steal again."

"I promise, daddy," she said through tears.

"You know that the boys will be listening for your cries when I spank you. I will hit my knee and you yell and scream, ok?"

What an actress she is, thought Marco, as she howled. When she arrived in the kitchen all in tears, Kitty was very upset. She followed her to her bedroom and asked:

"Show Mommy where Daddy hit you, my poor darling?"

Cunningly Johnna said, "No, Mommy. I must pay for stealing like a good Ukrainian farmer's wife would. I promised Daddy that I would never steal again." Later that night Kitty told Marco what had happened when she asked to see where her father had beat her. What an actress she is, thought Marco.

"That's my little girl," he said with a knowing smile.

When Johnna was in the Third Grade, another incident happened. Only this time Mark bore the brunt. There was a black boy named Henry who was in Grade Seven with him. One day in the schoolyard, Johnna came up to him and began singing,

"Nigger, nigger, pull the trigger. Bang! Bang! Bang!"

Henry ran after her but the bell rang and he couldn't catch her. Johnna had come home on the first bus and Mark, who had stayed for sports came on the last bus. When he walked into the kitchen, one eye closed and bleeding badly Kitty asked,

"Oh my God, Mark! Whatever happened to you?"

"Johnna called Henry a nigger and because he couldn't catch her he beat me up instead," wailed Mark.

Marco who was standing by, knew that this time he would have to use the strap on Johnna. On their way to the shed, he said,

"Well, young lady, you are not going to be a good Ukrainian farmer's wife after all! You stole Matthew's coin collection, you ridiculed Luke for his weaknesses and now you showed a great lack of respect for Henry because his skin is a different colour. You are disrespectful of others, of their feelings and of their property."

"What do you mean dis-res-pect-ful, Daddy?"

"Well when you respect a person like Henry or Luke, you don't make fun of them because they are different. If you respect someone you also respect their property, like Matthew's coin collection."

"I see, Daddy. That's what Sister Helen meant when she said, "Do unto others as you want them to do to you. Isn't it?"

"Yes and I am sure that you understand now. But you must pay for hurting others. You can't get the coins back. You can't undo the picture you drew of Luke and you can't uncall Henry names. But tomorrow you will tell Henry, Mark and Luke that you are sorry and promise never to hurt them again."

Marco gave Johnna a walloping neither of them would ever forget. Her tears were not pretend and the marks inflicted often reminded her of her failures until they healed.

The three brothers were not as forgiving and they waited patiently for an opportunity to get even with their sister. It came when Johnna was in Grade Four. They intercepted a love letter that she had written to Alan Forrest who was in Grade Five. They framed it and put it up in the living room for all to see. They guarded it well and took shifts to make sure she didn't get it down. On several occasions, they caught her sneaking down at night, to get to it. She couldn't get it off the wall and no matter how much she cried about it, Marco and Kitty said that she got what she deserved. Johnna surely felt over-punished, especially at Christmas when the whole family visited. But the puppy love flourished in spite of it all.

Alan Forrest, whose father owned the jewelry shop and the precious stones mine and quarry, was one year older than Johnna. He was tall for his ten years and very, very handsome. They soon began doing things together, like fishing, playing baseball or hide-and-seek. They spent hours birdwatching or just exploring the countryside together. Kitty often spoke to Marco about it. As the years passed, Kitty began to worry more and more about this relationship.

"It isn't normal for her to spend so much time with Alan, Marco. She should be spending more time with girls of her own age! Every time I speak to her about it, she says girls are so boring. I think we should consider sending her to boarding school with the sisters in Winnipeg, where I went. Don't you?"

"I'll think about it. Now that Matthew is in the Air Force, we have to hire a man to replace him and that eats into our overhead. I seriously don't think we can afford it."

The British Commonwealth Plan had chosen Souris for one of its Air Force training schools. Matthew had joined up while he was still in high school. It was nice to have him so near but the Rymhs realized that there would be other airmen coming into Souris also. They decided that they would make the sacrifice necessary to send Johnna to boarding school and away from these influences. To that effect, Kitty wrote to Sister Alice to ask if they would accept Johnna at a reduced rate for the year. She was overjoyed when the answer came back that she would be accepted at $300 a year instead of the annual $500. Only then did they tell Johnna. If she ever resented being sent away, she never said. Kitty knew that she was too curious not to go along with it.

There was no ceremony for passing from elementary school, but there was always a party. This year it was a hayride and it would end up at Lily Dodd's, where a campfire rose into the evening sky and food had been set up. There would be dancing on the recently constructed outdoor floor. Johnna was overjoyed when Alan asked her to be his date. She answered with a giggle, because she had never been on a "date" with him. They had spent plenty of time together but this was different. It was so grown-up like!

The June evening was warm and brightly lit by a full moon. They sang and laughed and chatted as the wagon sped down the country roads. At Lily's, benches had been set up around the huge bonfire. Opposite the dance floor, a huge table had been decked with mountains of food. The ladies were serving and the men were cooking hot dogs and corn on the cob.

As Alan and Johnna sat around the fire, he brought her a coke. She tasted it and gagged as she spat it out.

What's this Alan? It tastes awful!"

"It's just a little rum to loosen you up a bit. After a couple of sips you get used to it and it makes you feel mellow. It's the grown-up thing to do at a party."

Alan was already going into Grade Ten. He must know these things, thought Johnna so she went along with it.

"Let's dance," said Alan.

"But Alan, I don't know how to dance!"

"Have another coke. I'll show you how. All you have to do is listen to the music and let me lead you."

Soon they were on the dance floor and the coke had helped Johnna lose all her inhibitions and fears. The song was slow and mellow. Alan held Johnna very close and whispered the words in her ear, kissing it gently as he did.

"I'll be loving you, always. With a love that's true, always. Days may not be fair, always. That's when I'll be there, always."

Strange new feelings ran through Johnna's body. She assumed that it must be the rum and coke. All evening every time they danced or Alan was close, those same strange feelings ran through her and made her shiver in spite of the June heat.

After several dances, Alan suggested that they go for a walk. She welcomed the suggestion because she was hot and sweaty. They walked down to the fields behind the barn and sat under a huge tree. The large silver moon was low on the horizon. Suddenly, Alan grabbed Johnna and began kissing her, long and hard. Soon his tongue caressed her inner mouth and those strange feelings welled up in her again and her body heaved up towards him. She felt so good that she didn't want it to stop when he pulled away.

"I love you Johnna," Alan said huskily between kisses that were more rapid and longer. "Let me prove it to you."

"My God!" thought Johnna. "This is just like it happens in my Harlequin novels!"

She was a bit too drunk to realize what was happening. Before she knew it, Alan had lowered her panties and was inside her, heaving up and down with growing speed.She was swept away into an unreal world until the pain became so intense that it sobered her up immediately.

"Stop, Alan! Stop! It hurts too much." she screamed.

She shot up, pulled up her panties and saw the blood. Alan tried to comfort her and assured her that it only hurts the first time and it won't bleed next time.

"How do you know that? You must have done it before," she wailed.

Alan didn't answer, he just reached for her, but she pulled away. When she realized what had happened, she felt miserable and confused. Ignoring Alan's pleas to wait, she ran back to the party and began mingling with the others. Mark noticed that she was acting strangely and he kept his eye on her for the rest of the evening and waited to go home with her.

Johnna's first sexual experience left her wondering why it felt so good and so awful at the same time. It didn't seem to hurt Alan. It would be many, many years before Johnna would experience how different sex is, when the love response is mutual. In the meantime she had to live with her guilt and her shame.

# Chapter Four

"Well, how is boarding school?" asked Marco, when he picked Johnna up at the train station.

"Nothing like home, Dad!" she said as she hugged him.

What Johnna didn't tell him was how she had missed Alan, nor how eager she was to see him again. The Christmas break was two weeks long and she was going to enjoy it to the hilt!

Matthew was still in England awaiting repatriation. He had been in the Air Force less than two years when the war ended. Mark had worked with his dad after graduation. With only Luke in school it was easier to keep Johnna in boarding school. When Kitty saw her, she knew that she had changed. As the holiday wore on, it was even more evident. She had learned to chip in and do her share of the chores without being asked. She wasn't overeager to be off somewhere all the time and seemed content to stay at home. She wasn't less curious but she was more discreet and caring.

"When can I go into town, Mom?" she asked the day after her arrival.

"Why, Mark has to go in today, so you can go with him. Go and visit Granddad. He is so lonely without Granny."

After visiting her grandfather, she popped into Forrest's Jewellers.

"Good morning, Mrs. Forrest. How are you?"

"Why Johnna dear, I'm fine. I'm a bit tired. Mr. Forrest is not well and I had to take over the store. I'm eager for Alan to be home, to help in the shop so I can get ready for Christmas. He should be in from Winnipeg tomorrow."

"Winnipeg? I thought that he had gone to Brandon High?"

"He did in Grade Nine. But for whatever reasons, late in August he changed his mind and went to a boarding school in Winnipeg."

"I didn't know that. Please greet Mr. Forrest and Alan when he comes home."

"I will dearie," she said as she patted Johnna's hand affectionately.

How she wished that Alan would marry that girl. Mr. Forrest was worried about her religion but not her. She wanted only the best for her only son and she wanted him happy above all else. Two days later Johnna met Alan in her grandfather's former store. He was more handsome than she remembered.

"Hi," she said. "I didn't know that you were in Winnipeg too. Why did you change? I thought you liked it at Brandon?"

"Hi. Would you believe me if I said I wanted to be closer to you? I thought you were still mad at me. At least I got to see you at the sports events."

"Really and you didn't speak to me?"

"You were with a crowd of gals and guys and I didn't want to interrupt."

"I can't believe it! Don't ever do that again! At least you can greet me."

Their eyes locked and she had that funny feeling run through her body again and her heart skipped a beat. Now at least she knew why it happened and she knew how to shield herself from her emotions.

"Are you going to the Christmas dance?" Alan asked hopefully.

"I'd love to but Christmas is sacrosanct at our house and it is a family affair."

Johnna wanted so much to invite him to her house, but she knew that her parents would not accept a stranger at the family gathering. Also she realized that his mother needed him so much, especially at Christmas. What she couldn't accept however was that she had heard that he had already asked Lily Dodds to the dance.

When she met him in town after Christmas, that old funny feeling was gone. No more rivers of shivers she thought.

"Would you like a coke?" he asked.

"Sorry, Alan, but I must visit my grandfather," she lied.

She believed him when he said that he loved her at the hayride. She also believed him when he said that he would never love another. Now she wasn't even sure that she loved him!

"Another time then," he said as he sauntered away.

Johnna felt a tear fall down her cheek. Why was it so hard to build relationships? Why can't we be friends like we were when we were kids? Why had that strange warm feeling disappeared? Why do I feel that he doesn't love me anymore? Am I jealous of Lily Dodds? She remembered what Sister Margaret had said in Religion Class. "It takes time to build love. One mustn't mistake chemistry between a man and a woman for love. That is sex and it is only part of it. Two people must build trust and respect between them. To build a lasting relationship takes a lot of unselfishness and hard work by both parties." Had it just been chemistry between her and Alan? How do you make another person understand how you feel? Johnna wondered. She spoke to her mom about these things and was really surprised at how much she knew and understood. It created a new bond between them.

Back at boarding school, she started to attend sporting events in the hope of meeting Alan. In Souris, on holidays she made every effort to meet him as often as possible but the old feeling just wasn't there. They were friends but there was no more magic between them. In her final year, she invited Alan to be her date at her graduation prom. He had accepted from Brandon College where he was getting his first degree before entering the University of Toronto School of Architecture.

He came to pick her up at the convent school where she had spent the better part of the last four years. His heart beat wildly as she came down the oak stairs in the foyer of Madonna Hall. She had indeed become a very beautiful woman. Her cornflower blue organdy dress accentuated her blue eyes. Her long black hair highlighted her alabaster-like skin. "I must have her," thought Alan.

The dance had been magical for them both.

"Johnna, you know that I have loved for a long time. Tonight, I realized that you mean more to me than life itself. Will you marry me?"

"Oh Alan! I love you too, but I am not ready for marriage yet. There's so much that I want to do before I settle down. I want to go to college. I want to be a teacher."

"You can do that as my wife. You won't have to worry about anything. I'll have a cook and a housekeeper for you. You'll be free to study."

"No, Alan. When I marry, I want to have children. I want to be a full-time wife and mother."

"Are you sure you won't change your mind? Maybe your dad won't be able to afford college expenses. You would never have to worry as Mrs. Alan Forrest."

With the same faith that her mother had, she said, "God will provide, if it's meant to be. I am really flattered. However if I attended the university as missus, it would restrict my experiences and interactions, which are so much a part of campus life. I would miss the camaraderie among singles that is so enriching. No, Alan. I must get my degree and teaching certificate first."

"I respect you for sticking to your guns as it were, but will you do me one favour for old times sake? Come and spend the night with me in town tonight? I have reservations at the Fort Garry Hotel. Let me show you how much I do love you."

"Oh Alan! I'm not thirteen anymore! I didn't know better then but I know the possible consequences now. I will make you a promise though. I will never marry another man, I promise!"

Alan left her at the door, promising to wait for her as long as it took.

Back home, Johnna seemed very pensive and quiet. Her parents wondered if anything had happened the night of the prom. At supper one evening Kitty asked her if she had decided what she would do in the fall.

"I want to teach secondary school. Alan proposed to me on the night of the prom but I told him that I wasn't ready for marriage."

"Surely, you wouldn't consider marrying a non-Catholic?"

"If I loved him enough I would. You married one and it worked out just fine."

"Wouldn't you want to marry a good Ukrainian farmer." interjected Marco.

"Maybe after I have taught a few years. I want to teach secondary school and that means at least four years of university. Do you suppose that we can afford it, Dad?"

"I'd love to say yes, but with Luke going to Veterinary College and Matthew talking marriage, that leaves only Mark on the ranch. It depends on how many hired hands I'll need. We'll see. We'll see."

In her last year of high school, Johnna felt called to the religious life. She thought of becoming a sister with the Holy Spirit Missionaries with whom she had studied. She was really struggling with her decision and Alan's offer hadn't helped. She liked Alan but was not sure that it was love. She wondered if she only thought of entering because her education would be assured. What guarantee would she have that they would let her prepare to teach high school? It was known among the students that they would have to fill their obligations to the diocese with regards to postings and that may not be at the secondary level. Sister Margaret, whom they all loved had been transferred to teach Grade Three in one of their schools. The students had resented her leaving. The more she prayed for guidance the more confused she got.

One morning she rose at the crack of dawn and made her way down to the river. Like her dad she came here to think and pray. She could talk out loud, yell or cry and no one would hear her. It was an ideal place for a spiritual combat! The conclusion that she reached was very simple. If she didn't try she would never find peace.

At breakfast she told her parents of her decision. Kitty was thrilled and Marco was stunned. He had never even thought of that possibility.

"When?" he asked.

"The entry date is August the fifteenth. I have already contacted the Mother General in Toronto and am just waiting for an answer."

"Toronto? Why so far away? Aren't there any barracks closer by?" Marco asked as though it were the army.

"Oh Dad! Just think no one else will have your little princess," Johnna said trying to console him.

"I've only had you for seventeen years and poof it's all up in smoke!"

"The training is at the Mother House of the Holy Spirit Missionaries in Toronto. It lasts two years and if I am accepted, I will take my first vows for three years. Then if I still want to stay and they still want me, I will make Final Vows. So you see, there is plenty of time for permanent decisions."

"When the hell do you get your degree? asked Marco worried.

"That's all I can tell you now, because that's all I know."

Things that she had heard the sisters talk about like commitment, service, and love of the poor that their Foundress was known for; poverty, chastity and obedience were all nebulous even to her. One of the sisters had talked about leaving the world. Johnna wondered where they went. It was all so mysterious. What had attracted her to this particular congregation was its devotion to the poor that had been its raison d'être from its founding. Johnna had toyed with the idea of being a nurse so she could work among the poor. These sisters also had missions in Africa which had great appeal to Johnna.

The first two years of novitiate training were difficult for Johnna. She had to have reasons for doing everything. This was contrary to the spirit of blind obedience, where one never questioned a command. There were stories of some novices who were told to go and plant carrots upside down. The obedient ones did without question! Johnna was only glad that she had not been asked that. She had experiences in replanting carrots but not upside down! Every new candidate chose a Father Confessor to whom she could go for advice, in the confessional, of course! These Holy Spirit Fathers had been associated with this community since it was their Founding Father who had guided their foundress, Mother Celeste to begin the community. He had also asked her to send sisters to teach and nurse in Africa. The man Johnna chose had been a missionary in Africa and he was practical with a modern outlook on life.

She went to him one day, and told him that she was doubting whether or not she belonged in the convent. Thoughts of Alan filled all her waking hours when she wasn't occupied and also her dreams at night. The good Father listened patiently then said,

"Maybe you are right and maybe it's just a temptation. You know that the devil knows that with your determination and generous spirit you could do a lot of good in Africa. On the other hand it may be that the good you are to do may be back in the world. Now is the time of discernment. Time and prayer are the only ways to obtain true discernment. I have a plan for you. I want you to write in your little black book that you call your "Conscience", how many times you think of this young man every day. Never mind the nights, that's only the activity of your subconscious mind. When you come to confession next week, you just start off by saying how many times and I will know who it is. I want you to do this for a couple of months. Is that understood?"

"Yes Father," she replied and left.

The first week that Johnna returned to the confessional, it was seventy-eight times. The following week, fifty-four. Finally at the end of two months Alan no longer came into her thoughts, night or day.

Of the forty-three girls who had entered her group, only twenty-two took their First Vows. Johnna started her university training in September, 1952. Her companion was her good friend from Winnipeg, Sister Irene Kendall.

# Chapter Five

First Vows day had come and gone. The newly professed sisters had had their holiday-break and the official postings called nominations, would be announced tomorrow. The young nuns affectionately called these placements, their "marching orders". At breakfast, Johnna and Irene each had a note on their plate; "Please report to the Mother General's office at 9:30 a.m. today." They had had a few such requests over the past two years. Like the time that they hitch-hiked back from the zoo or the time they picked apples from the orchard without asking. They had not been pleasant encounters. The mother general, Mother Judith, wanted the novices to learn what was expected of them. The penalties she meted out were more humiliating than physically hurtful; the sting of the reproach was the truth of it. Understandably they went with apprehension to this meeting. As they waited in the outer office to be called in, their nervousness was visible. Irene tapped a foot nervously to the beat of the clock which seemed louder because of the oak panelling and the profound silence. Johnna lifted and dropped the huge rosary that hung from a black leather belt at her waist. Each was lost in thought, when a soft voice interrupted their reveries.

"Reverend Mother will see you now."

"It can't be all that bad, since we've been called in together," Johnna whispered through clenched teeth, as they slipped through the door. They performed the usual ritual of kneeling and waiting to be spoken to.

"Come Holy Spirit," Reverend Mother chanted.

"And fill our hearts with Thy love," they responded as they took the seats before her desk.

"I hope you weren't too frightened at being called before the high throne," she said with a smile. "It isn't bad news this time. In fact it is very good news. Our sisters have always been internally trained to teach by the older sisters. This however, only allowed them to teach in our convent schools and not in the diocesan schools. Now, the Archbishop has asked us to begin teaching in the inner city, where many of our Catholic immigrants live. Government regulations are very stringent today. In the old days, a few of our sisters went to Normal School as the teacher-training was called and they in turn trained the others. All one needed to get into Normal School was a High School Certificate."

"But the Normal Schools are being phased out," added Johnna.

"That's right Sister. So the General Council has decided to send the two of you to the university to get a degree in education. Your names were mentioned as possible candidates many times and I finally approved the choice."

"Wow," said Johnna smiling at Irene, who was too stunned to talk.

"You will begin classes in a few weeks. Hopefully, with summer school sessions, you can graduate in three years instead of four. You will move into our house in Rosedale where Sister Caroline, the superior, will be your guide and your mentor. As you know she has a degree from McGill in Montreal. She will give you all the directives you need as she has been briefed by our General Council. She will arrange for a car to take you to and from classes every day. Are there any questions?"

"Yes, Mother. Why can't we use the Toronto Transit Corporation? The TTC would be much cheaper and there will be many days when we will need to do library research. It would be difficult to tell the driver at what time we would be ready."

"Good idea, Sister Johnna. Speak to Sister Caroline about it before classes begin."

Mother Judith loved Johnna. How many women possess imagination, delicacy, zest and fire? She regarded the comments in her file as perverse satisfaction and petty jealousies. She promised herself that she would protect her as long as she was the Mother General.

"May the Holy Spirit fill you hearts with love," Mother Judith said in dismissal.

"Amen," they answered in unison and left.

Once outside the office, the new students looked at each other and with a high five said,

"Yes!"

"There's always a fly in the ointment, though," commented Johnna.

"How do you mean?" Irene queried.

"I'll be at loggerheads with "Caro" all the time. Last spring when I did my novice-practicum and stayed in residence at her house, we never saw eye to eye on anything. The sisters explained to me why they thought she was like that. When she was a teenager her brother drowned in a fishing accident and they never found the body. The following year they found her father's drowned body. Then a few years later they had to put her mother in a mental institution. That certainly was enough trauma for any teenager."

"Oh, how awful!"

"Well that explains why she's so strange but it doesn't make it any easier for her subjects. I wish Mother Judith would have let us stay at the Mother House. I get such bad vibes from that lady!"

Settling in at the Rosedale convent was easier than both young sisters had expected. In fact, Caroline was all sugar and spice. But Johnna knew from bitter experience that it was just the calm before the storm. If you weren't a "yes" person, who agreed with all her idiosyncrasies, you were an outcast and she made life miserable for you. Johnna thought of her mother, now widowed, who said often in her letters that she was lucky because in the convent she had nothing to suffer. Oh, what illusions the laity had!

Three days after their arrival they were summoned before Caroline. Johnna stopped by at the chapel to beg God to keep her calm and respectful. She asked for the grace to do all Caro's biddings. She really wanted to get along with her.

Seated stiffly at her mahogany desk, Sister Caroline began,

"Sisters, you realize that you are the first sisters in this diocese to attend the university. Your religious garb will make you stick out like sore thumbs. Every action, every word that you utter will be scrutinized. Enemies of our faith will ferret out any deviation from what you proclaim by your religious profession. You will stay together at all times to avoid being maligned."

"Ye gads," thought Johnna humorously to herself, "I've always gone potty alone."

She often went off on these mental tangents—it was her way of keeping her sanity and not getting into trouble. Some of these authorities figures rambled on so!

"You will be driven to the university and picked up each day by the convent driver. You will bring a bag lunch but will be given a small weekly stipend for emergencies. Books, binders, field trips and such will be billed to me for payment. Now, are there any questions?"

"Yes, Sister. What happens when we need to do research in the library?"

"Well, Sister Johnna, you tell me the night before and I'll make arrangements with the driver."

"In the spirit of our Foundress, wouldn't it be cheaper and more in keeping with the spirit of poverty for us to take public transport?" Johnna queried.

"Sister, do not confuse the spirit of poverty with poverty of spirit. Our Foundress, Mother Celeste, placed poverty of spirit, this willingness to let the authorities decide what is best for us far above the other."

"I can't believe that Mother Celeste praised dim-wittedness as a virtue! Surely to be poor means to live like the poor as much as possible without hindering our work. That is what attracted me to this congregation, to work with and for the poor. That is why I want to go to Africa and work with the poorest of the poor someday."

"I appreciate your sentiments, Sister, but you have also taken a vow of obedience and it is just as important as the vow of poverty. Doing things the way your superiors suggest is just as virtuous. Tomorrow morning, the car will take you to the university for Orientation Day. If there are no further questions you may leave."

After the students had left, Sister Caroline got out Johnna's file and entered yet another insubordination. At the same time she thought that Sister Irene should get praise for her humility in accepting what the authorities asked of her and that was so noted on her file. "Brownie points" Johnna would undoubtedly call them.

The Orientation Day for new students was held in Hart House. A young man came up behind Johnna and placed his hands to cover her eyes and said,

"Guess who?"

Luke, who had just completed his two-year pre-veterinary training in May, had come to surprise Johnna. And surprise he did! Spontaneously she turned around and hugged and kissed him effusively.

She had forgotten her religious decorum to the delight of everyone nearby. Poor Luke was very embarrassed.

"My baby sister," he said apologetically."

The day passed very quickly. The car was to meet them at three o'clock. It was three forty-five when they arrived at the rendezvous.

"It's about time. We've been waiting forty-five minutes. Is that what an education does for you? It makes you selfish and inconsiderate of others," one of the sisters said.

The two students made no answer. They had been warned by the Superior General that this might happen. Their silence did not make the resentment towards them go away but it gave them peace. All this could be avoided, thought Johnna if we travelled via the TTC.

One day in April, Luke invited Johnna and Irene to have lunch with him at his apartment. It was close to the campus, he assured them and they would be on time for their afternoon lectures. They told the cook, in the evening, that they had not eaten their lunches that day and would take them tomorrow. The cook, over-zealous about their health reported to the Superior that they had not eaten their lunch. She in turn called them in for an explanation after evening prayers.

"Sisters, please explain why you did not eat your lunch today," she said sternly.

"We had lunch at my brother's apartment," Johnna said.

"You WHAT?" queried Sister Caroline.

Johnna repeated her statement.

"That my dear sisters, is a very serious breach of rule! I can't believe that you would do that without permission. For your penance, you will avow this publicly at the annual retreat at the Mother House in August. You may be excused."

Once outside, Johnna said, "I never even thought about it. How did you feel about it, Renie?"

"I enjoyed the meal as well as the regurgitations," she said with a laugh.

Johnna had been saving all her stipend money and when she had enough she purchased a leather pencil case at the bookstore. She was forever losing pens and pencils as she went from class to class and nine dollars didn't seemed too extravagant. That night however Caroline called for her and queried it. She went on and on at how

Johnna had failed in poverty this time. Johnna began to laugh. She was nearly in tears as she sat before the superior.

A mystified Sister Caroline asked, "What is so funny, Sister?"

"Well," said Johnna. "You are sitting behind a mahogany desk, in a stuffed leather armchair, in your luxurious office. You have a thermo fax, a Xerox duplicator, a coloured T.V., an electric typewriter, and a lazy-boy. It all seems so incongruous."

"All this was given to me by the father of one of my students."

"So if someone had given me the pencil case I would have been poor? But because I frugally saved my stipends to buy it, I failed in poverty?"

The superior was visibly shaken by the encounter and she excused Johnna from her presence. Johnna waited for further repercussions but they never came.

On June 1st, 1955, the two sisters graduated "cum laude", with a degree in education. There would be no more summer school for them. After a retreat they would pronounce Final Vows and receive their first teaching assignment in inner city Toronto. Johnna could hardly wait to start teaching. She was born to it, she thought.

# Chapter Six

Although Johnna had a verbal promise from the Mother General that she would be sent to Africa one day, she was realistic enough to know that there were no such assurances in the religious life. So she lived in the present and made the best of each day. In her heart she sang along with Doris Day, "Whatever will be, will be, The future's not ours to see, Que sera, sera."

"Her teaching career began at Dominic Savio School, in the Queen-Spadina area of Cabbage Town, as the area was fondly called. She had been assigned to teach the First and Second Grades combined, much to her dismay. She said to Renie one day,

"I don't understand it. I've always told the superiors that I wanted to teach High School and you've always told them that you didn't think you could handle the older kids. Do you think that they have done this purposefully to "break our wills" as they always say?"

"I have no doubt. It's their way of breaking our will. Who knows? I know that I'm going to have a hard time with the older kids. They frighten me and I am so shy that they will take advantage of me I am sure."

There were forty-nine pupils in Johnna's class. What she called her 'wall-to-wall' kids. The youngest one was Alphonso, the eldest of five children. He was very small, wore glasses and spoke through his nose which made his speech slurred and slow. His mother was so busy with the other children that he often had to fend for himself. Johnna's oldest student was Tony. He was tall and sportif. Being the youngest of a family of seven made him worldly-wise and at fourteen very mature compared to his classmates. One day Johnna told the children the story of creation during the religion class. When the story was finished, Alphonso raised his hand to ask a question.

"Yes, Alphonso."

"Thister, where do I come from? How was I made?" Before Johnna had a chance to answer, Tony was on his feet and from the back of the class said,

"I'll tell him sister. I know where babies come from."

"Sit down, Tony," Johnna said sternly, "He didn't ask you!"

Johnna proceeded to explain that every living thing starts with a seed.

"The seed that started you, Alphonso, was in your mommy's tummy, and..."

Tony shot up again. "I know how the seed got into his mommy's tummy! I can tell him."

At that moment, the recess bell rang and Tony grabbed the soccer ball and was out the door. Much to Johnna's relief!

"Whew! Saved by the bell!" said Johnna as she made her way to the staff room. The staff enjoyed her telling of the recent episode that had happened just before the bell.

Johnna was so busy, that the days literally flew by. Every evening, she meticulously prepared the twenty-nine writing exercises in the Grade One notebooks. She made copies of seatwork for the various groups in Reading and Arithmetic. Those were the days when duplication was done on gelatin slates, using a purple pencil. It was a slow and shoddy process and consumed a lot of time but with so many children and so many groups, everyone had to be kept busy. Johnna seemed to be a natural for teaching and she handled the discipline like a pro. When she went to bed at nine-thirty every evening, she fell like a sack of potatoes until five-twenty in the morning when the rising bell woke her from a sound sleep. She was very happy and couldn't believe how much she enjoyed the little ones.

Late in November, the principal announced at lunch that the inspector would be in the following Monday.

"I don't want to frighten the new teachers, but he usually spends more time in your classes. He is very fussy about your daily preparation book and your class registers. Just make sure that these are up to date and also have a true seating plan available."

Johnna remembered from Teachers' College, that they had to write out every lesson plan, every day. She had been too busy to be strict with hers. She would have to spend the week-end putting her notes up to date!

All week-end, she wrote and wrote and wrote until everything was up to date and she could at last relax. It was so much against the grain for her to go so much into detail using precious time that could be used for other things, instead of on useless conventions. On Monday morning at nine o'clock there was a knock at her door. In walked the principal followed by the inspector. After the introductions, the visitor found himself a seat at the back of the room and told Johnna to carry on. She was taking Arithmetic and the little First Graders were learning to count to ten. In those days there was no universal kindergarten and no TV so children came to school with very little basic learning.

The inspector began walking around, checking exercise books wending his way to the front of the class. Once there, he asked if anyone could count for him. Eager little hands went up; there was no lack of choice. Then the inspector asked if there was anyone who could count from ten to zero. There were no takers. Then a small hand shot up.

The inspector smiled at Johnna, who said, "Yes, Victor."

He started counting from ten backwards. When he got to zero, he continued, "One in the hole, two in the hole, three in the hole, etc."

The two adults had a great laugh. The inspector then asked Victor if his teacher had taught him that.

"No," he answered, "my mom and dad play cards and when they lose they go in the hole!"

The inspector's visit had come and gone without a glitch. Every day there was a number of pupils who waited until four-thirty for the bus to pick them up during which time every teacher supervised her own pupils in their respective classes. In Johnna's classroom there was a piano. This one day, little Marilyn asked Johnna to play 'Chop Sticks' with her. Johnna couldn't get the hang of it. The little six-year-old looked up at her with disgust and said,

"How can you be so big and so stupid!"

Out of the mouths of babes, come words of truth, Johnna said as she looked at her big farmers' fingers.

Little Victor, of inspector fame, raised his hand one day in class to ask a question. Johnna had been very patient with him and his problem of stuttering and he had gained enough confidence to read out loud and even ask questions, much to the delight of his parents.

"Sss-iss-ter," he blurted out, Wi,wi,will you wait for me to grow up so I can mar-ry you?"

"Of course Victor. But you had better hurry up, because I can't wait forever," she laughed.

The professors at the university had often lectured about the difficulties that new Canadians have in learning English, because they only spoke it at school. Johnna often heard expressions such as, "Hey shister, he gots my pencil", or "This isa my pencil." Johnna had immense patience and really enjoyed all the extra preparation that it demanded of her. That is until she attended her first Teachers' Catholic Union Meeting where the salaries were an item on the agenda. She learned that the Sisters were paid $500 dollars a year, whereas the Brothers were paid twenty-five hundred! When Johnna asked the chairman why the disparity, the Chairman said that the Brothers needed more money; they had expenses, like cigarettes, sports events and entertainment like films etc. Johnna was livid when the men rudely laughed.

Upon returning home she took the issue up with the Superior who was indignant that she should query the decision of the Archbishop who set these regulations up with the approval of the General Council of the congregation.

"It is not just. The Sisters are the ones who do most of the work; they never get to be principals and they are paid one-quarter of the salary!"

The Superior said, "Sister Johnna, do you eat less, are you poorly housed or clothed; do you not have all the material things that you need?"

She shocked Sister Caroline deeply when she said, "But I can☐t go to the movies, or to a hockey game or buy cigarettes!"

It didn't take long after Johnna's departure that the file came out and another addition was made. Criticizing administrative decisions even at the highest diocesan level would drive the nails deep into Johnna's religious-life coffin!

Life went on. Johnna worked hard and succeeded well in spite of the Superior's hopes. Johnna was determined to be the best of herself and use the gifts that the Lord had bestowed on her. Being true to herself, as her father had always taught her, was to her being Christ-like. She never wavered or compromised herself; her sense of justice precluded petty jealousies that would always plague her because she was unafraid to be forthright and she was as straight as an arrow. She called a spade a spade.

In May, an incident occurred that caused her to come to loggerheads with Caro again. The Grade Two pupils were making their First Holy Communion. Directives from the Chancery had insisted that the pupils bring a Baptismal Certificate before being allowed to receive the Sacrament of the Eucharist. One particular student, Paulus Fellacino had not yet brought his certificate. Johnna had told Auturo Fellacino, the child's father that he must produce the document or Paulus would not be allowed to join his friends for the ceremony.

That evening, Arturo arrived at the convent and asked to see Sister Johnna. When she entered the parlour, he handed her a bouquet of flowers, a basket of fruits and several boxes of chocolates for 'the good sisters'.

Johnna thanked him and asked if she could help him.

"Well, yes you can Sister. You see when my restaurant burned down, we were living above it and we lost all our documents, including Paulus' baptismal certificate. I swear on my mother's grave that he was baptized at St. Maria Goretti Church.

"Then, Mr. Fellacino just go to the parish church and they will make a duplicate copy for you."

"You see I am a very, very busy man and I just don't have time. Why don't you just believe me?" he said as he caressed her sensually with his eyes.

"I'm sorry," Johnna said returning his advances with scorn, "I cannot do that."

"Then, may I see the Sister Superior alone?" he asked.

Johnna never knew exactly what had transpired but she was still adamant when Caroline called her in later that night.

"Sister Johnna, Mr. Fellacino is very upset because of your stubbornness and has revoked his promise to buy new drapes for our newly decorated chapel. That represents thousands of dollars. Can you not make a compromise here?"

"I will not be bought. If it were poor little Alphonso's mother making that request you would be the first to refuse her. No, I'm sorry I cannot compromise myself. If he wishes, he can go to the bishop. Seriously I don't think the boy was ever baptized or it would be a simple matter to get a copy of the baptismal certificate from Maria Goretti Church."

After Johnna left, Caroline went to the file and entered another incident of "gross insubordination". Another nail in her coffin.

In the three years that Johnna stayed at the Rosedale Convent, her personal file accumulated many pages. At every annual retreat, Mother Judith praised her work, totally ignoring the file comments that were sent to her annually. Every year she told her to prepare for work in the mission field and never admonished her for her so-called insubordination. She had a good understanding of human nature and read beyond these derogatory comments. Nonetheless, this remained a blot on her reputation for the duration of her religious life. The information was misused by petty, jealous authorities who did not have the ability to sift though and see the true potential of this very capable woman. Because they were not able to make their own judgment they relied on the past and it created conflicts that never would have otherwise occurred.

Because Mother Judith was a fine judge of character, she considered the women who wrote these biased reports and she chose to ignore them. She knew from her experience that really great women were always criticized, even as she was herself, and that the work of the Lord went beyond all our human frailties. Little did she realize, however, that in the mission field these comments would be interpreted to the letter and usually totally out of context. She realized that Johnna would have difficulty but she believed that she would be able to handle it. She had chosen her to go to the missions because she needed someone that would be working with and for these poor people. She didn't need any more "niche-builders". On her visitations, she had seen men and women, starting out ever so sincerely and after time, building bastions of comfort amid the poverty that surrounded them. She had sent Johnna and Irene knowing that they would bring a new cooperation among the blacks, sisters and students alike. At the annual retreat in 1959, Mother Judith told the two young teachers that they would be going to teach at a girls' boarding school in Basutoland, South Africa. She gave them a real idea of what they would be faced with.

"Your biggest challenges will be with the whites, not the Africans. There are several social reasons for that. They are living in a foreign culture, strained by the political situation caused by apartheid. Apartheid is a political situation like no other in the world. Also the weather is hot and dry for ten or eleven months a year, with drought ever looming. This creates a nerve-racking situation for the so-called "Europeans" who are mainly used to four seasons. Isolation makes many seek compensations in ways that would not be acceptable in our own culture. For example, the good Fathers were taught in the novitiate training to make their own beds and keep their room tidy. Under guise of affording work for the Africans, they have their beds made, their rooms cleaned etc. The missionaries eventually live like the Boers, using the blacks as lackeys. It will be very difficult not to fall into a rut. It will be even more difficult not to criticize what you see. You counteract this by not doing it yourself; by being the servant not the one being served; by respecting the blacks as people equal to you before God. Their civilization is different from ours but it is not absent. Remember that you are bringing them education not civilization which they already have."

"Thank you, Mother. I will do my best with what God has given me" answered Johnna for both of them.

"Now you will go to the sewing room and the sisters there will make your dresses and prepare your trousseau for the missions. The Bursar General will see to your passport, your shots, and travelling documents. I will be at the airport to see you off. May the Holy Spirit fill your hearts with love."

"Amen," Johnna replied and left. It was still retreat, and she couldn't talk to Irene so she left her a note on her pillow in the dorm and all it said was, "Wow!" After a visit to her family and friends in Souris, Manitoba, Johnna spent a few days with Irene's family in Winnipeg. Back in Toronto, they finished packing their trunks and got their final shots. At a ceremony for departing missionaries, all the sisters bent and kissed their feet as the choir sang, "Blessed are the feet of those who bring the Good News to the poor".

After the ceremony, Johnna said to Irene,

"Boy was I tempted to kick Caroline in the teeth and say "Hypocrite!" to her when she kissed my feet."

"She would have run for your file and entered yet another incident of insubordination," laughed Irene.

On the twenty-fourth of September, 1959, the two new missioners boarded a KLM flight to Maseru, Basutoland via Amsterdam, Zurich, Rome, Brazzaville, and Johannesburg. Mother Judith feeling a great responsibility whispered to herself, as she watched the plane lift off "What have I done?"

# Chapter Seven

On the flight to Amsterdam, a stewardess approached the two sisters and gave them tourist brochures to peruse, saying,

"You have an eighteen hour wait in Amsterdam before your next flight. Let me know if there is anything you would like to see and KLM will make all the arrangements. It is a free service."

They began to study the pamphlets.

"The old port of Amsterdam has many ancient buildings, dating back to the 13th Century," read Johnna. "Why would we want to visit old buildings when we lived in one in Toronto for two years? Our Mother House is a museum!"

"Not quite six centuries old though. What I want to see, are the famous Ladies of the Night in the Red Light District where they sit in the windows luring customers," declared Irene.

"Yeah, me too. I would also love to visit a few of the twenty diamond cutting factories."

"Seriously, Johnna, I would just like to have a shower and a good sleep. I am totally zonked! I'm so exhausted from all the emotion and lack of sleep of the past few weeks!"

"Good idea. We'll tell her what our preference is."

They showered and slept in a beautiful room at the Schiphol Airport. After a long sleep, they had a meal and then had arranged to visit "The Van Gogh" and "The Rijks" museums. Back at the airport later they boarded their flight to Zurich. After an hour for refuelling, they took off for Rome where they had their dinner. They arrived at Kano, Nigeria the next morning. The café, was a lean-to set against the hanger cum baggage shed. The desert environment of blowing sand and camels passing by, gave it the look of a scene from a "Beau Geste" movie.

Their plane touched down at Brazzaville in the Belgian Congo at eleven p.m. The exterior temperature was well over a hundred degrees, so when the sisters emerged from the aircraft in their full habits, they literally wilted. All the starched items in their habits went limp and they felt that they had just come out of a pool. The short walk to the airport seemed like miles because they had to side-step the gekoes that carpeted the tarmac. These tropical lizards are quite harmless but walking on them in the middle of the night, is a whole new experience, which Johnna and Irene could not easily stomach.

Once inside the airport building, which was very hot and humid, Johnna asked a very short and very dark African in French and in English,

"Où sont les toilettes?, Where are the toilets?"

"Là", he pointed to a door.

The sisters headed for it, eager to see themselves in a mirror. As they entered, a white gentleman was washing his hands in the sink.

"Ooops, excusez-moi," Johnna said as she turned heel and bumped into a distracted Irene. "Wrong one", she told her bewildered mate.

She approached another waiter and asked in French again, "Où sont les toilettes pour dames?"

"Elles sont pour dames et messieurs."

"Now I remember Matthew telling us that in France the public toilets were for both sexes. I guess the Belgians also have the same customs."

"Let's forget it," said Irene, "You don't look so bad now that we are cooler. You just look like Saturday night after our basketball games in Toronto! Ask the waiter for some coffee."

"Deux tasses de café, s'il-vous-plaît," she asked another waiter.

The coffee arrived in two huge white cups. A very black man not five feet tall in a bright white uniform and a red fez, solemnly poured the thick syrupy liquid. Luckily their onward flight was called to board and they escaped this experience.

In the morning light, the green canopy of tropical forests looked like broccoli from above. The great rivers resembled ribbons of lasagna, in the rising sun. The East African mountains pierced the clouds that wrapped their lower flanks. They were awed by all the beauty that they drank in meditatively when the loudspeaker came on and broke their reverie.

This is the pilot. Look out on the right-hand side of the aircraft and you will see Kilimanjaro, Africa's highest mountain. It straddles the equator but it is perpetually covered in snow."

Irene snapped a photo that was later developed and became her great treasure.

At Jan Smuts Airport, in Johannesburg, they retrieved their luggage and checked in for the hour's flight to Maseru, the capital of Basutoland. They were met there by the African driver from their mission station in northern Basutoland. It was late afternoon when the ten-seater VW kombi arrived at Saint Joseph's Roman Catholic Mission at Khukhune. The mission compound was set in a rocky depression, surrounded by huge dongas and eroded plateaux. The conglomeration of buildings with their zinc and thatched roofs, rose out of the lowlands surrounding the Hololo River. The driver brought the kombi to a stop in front of a large u-shaped building of hewn sandstone. Ululations pierced the afternoon stillness as a crowd of black nuns greeted the two new arrivals from Canada. Johnna gave her usual, "Wow!"

Among the sea of black faces lost in the white robes of the Holy Spirit Missionaries, were four white faces, bronzed and withered by the sun and the hot, dry African winds. Johnna and Irene stepped out of the kombi. A tall, thin, ascetic-looking sister moved towards them and offered a bony hand and said,

"I am Sister Inez, the superior here at Saint Joseph's. In the name of all the staff, I welcome you both and wish you a happy stay here."

After each of the sisters was introduced, the group moved into the house.

As the two new sisters swish-swished along in their experimental terylene dresses, the African sisters giggled with delight.

Johnna immediately explained that they had been given this material because it was cool and very easy to wash and dry. They were the guinea pigs she explained. The Africans laughed because they took the expression literally.

At the door of the dinning room, Irene exclaimed,

"Look! Coca cola!"

"Wow!" Johnna used her usual expletive.

Sister Inez, at the head of the table, solemnly made the sign of the Cross and all the sisters sang it in Sesotho, their Bantu language.

"Ka laybitso lay Ntatay, lay la Moora, lay la Mooya, o halalaylang."

Three times they chanted, "In the name of the Father, and of the Son, and of the Holy Spirit. Amen." This was the traditional hymn that welcomed newcomers someone explained.

"I thought the traditional welcome was Khotso! Pula! Nala! Layshlohonolo!," said Johnna, "Peace, rain, abundance and blessings."

"That too," said Inez through pinched lips. "But the Christian one is the Sign of the Cross."

The evening passed quickly, as the newcomers shared news from Canada and answered a multitude of questions from every corner.

Turning to Irene, Inez said, "You will sleep in the main house. Sister Lucia will show you your room. Sister Jo-anna you will sleep in St. Bart's, the old rectory, where your classroom is. I will accompany you."

Johnna cringed at the mispronunciation of her name but refrained from commenting at this time. "I'm not going to get along with this lady!" she thought. Inez rose and motioned for Johnna to follow her. A couple of young sisters picked up her bags and followed. The generator had gone off, so it was very dark. Handing Johnna a flashlight she whispered,

"At night everyone carries a torch, especially to cross the thick, tall grasses in front of St. Bart's where snakes are known to take refuge. When the boarders arrive, they slash the grass and keep it short as a daily chore".

Entering the small bedroom, just off the classroom, Inez said,

"The cupboards are built into the mud walls. The mud is called local mud, and it's a mixture of clay and cow dung that becomes as hard as brick with time. The snakes, rats and mice eat their way through during the cold weather, so I would advise you to keep the doors closed and use the free-standing wardrobe for your clothes. On your table you have a candle and matches in case you have to get up during the night. The toilet is down the hall. The only tub is in the main building but hot water is brought from the kitchen every evening. There are many sand fleas which aren't so bad once they don't like your blood anymore. Well, goodnight and sleep well."

After Inez left there was an eerie silence. Johnna filled her basin with warm water from a matching enamel jug, which some kind soul had brought over for her. There was a matching enamel slop bucket with a lid for night use. Just as she finished her ablutions, she heard a gnawing noise which stopped her cold. She ignored it and jumped into her lumpy bed and fell asleep through sheer exhaustion and jet lag. In the wee hours of the morning, she was awakened by a crunching sound. Sitting up she lit her candle and listened. Where was it coming from? What was it? A snake? A rat? Fleas? The adrenalin flowed fast as she rose to investigate. Listening from different angles she realized that the sound came from the window. Moving cautiously nearer and nearer, she saw the forms of the cows silhouetted in the moonlight. They looked up at her nonchalantly as they munched the grass loudly. She laughed so loudly at herself that she frightened them away. Back in bed, she fell asleep again only to be awakened with a scratching at her door. She lit the candle and listened intently, then she heard a whisper,

"Mè it is time to get up" said a gentle voice at the door.

"But I just went to bed! What time is it?"

"It is five-thirty. Prayers start at six."

"Even during school holidays?"

"'Yes, Mè"

"Thank you. I am getting up."

Johnna splashed her face with the remaining water and dressed quickly. As she crossed the yard in the early morning light, she saw an arch before her. "That must be the chapel," she mused. Even in the chapel however, she still saw the arch before her. During the meditation time she slumbered; it was the only way to make the arch disappear. On the way to the refectory for breakfast, she followed Irene very closely, so she wouldn't go through "the mysterious arch". When she stepped on her heels, Irene turned sharply and screamed,

"Oh my God, Johnna! Your headgear is so far forward that we can't see your face." She pulled her into the pantry where they laughingly adjusted her coif.

"So, that's the mysterious arch that has been haunting me since I left my room. It was the edge of my coif that was so far forward, it looked like the end of a covered wagon."

Their laughter carried into the dining room where all the sisters waited silently for them. Inez said grace and they all sat down. Then she announced a day of recreation in honour of the new arrivals. It was a noisy meal as Johnna dramatized what had happened to her. After the meal the sisters filed out to go to their respective morning cleaning. Sister Inez waited for Johnna and Irene as they left the dinning room.

"Sisters, you are excused from cleaning this morning so you can unpack your steamer trunks that arrived last week."

"Wow, no cleaning," Johnna said sarcastically.

Later Johnna was in her classroom unpacking her trunk when Irene arrived.

"Haven't you finished yet?" asked Irene.

"No, I was looking at my pictures and I became nostalgic. There's one here of Alan Forrest and I at the graduation prom. It's hard to believe that it was nine years ago already. I wonder if he's married yet? I heard from my brother Luke that he works for an architectural firm in Toronto and is making a lot of money. I wonder if he would send me some to get a new mattress for my lumpy bed."

They both laughed. It was good to be just the two of them to share their impressions of their new surroundings.

"Gosh," said Irene, "Those Africans sure do make strange remarks!"

"How do you mean, Renie?"

"Well, Lucia told me that they call Inez, "Mooya" which means spirit or ghost, because she always turns up out of the blue and spooks everyone. She also said that it was a custom to give every white sister a name, so that when they talk about them, the whites won't understand who they are talking about."

"Why on earth would she tell you that, if it's supposed to be a native secret?"

"Maybe she's trying to get in good with me. You know a particular friendship or P.F. as we called them in the novitiate. Remember how the Mistress of Novices called them the curse of the religious life? I'll go along with her to find out what our Sotho name is."

"Be careful though. Watch for signs that you are getting in too deep."

"I already know what name they have for you. Although my Sesotho isn't too bright, I heard one of them say, "pompomnyanay" when you walked into the kitchen last night. When I asked Lucia what it meant she said simply "The beautiful one" and wrote it out for me in Sotho. She didn't even ask me why? Mine it appears is "Katse", the cat. She explained that it was used with Ma to distinguish it from the animal. So I am MaKatse."

"Gee. Our arrival surely has caused a stir. They continually laugh about us and say, "Swish, swish" when they see us because of our terylene dresses."

"I'll let you get on with your unpacking and see you at lunch."

Johnna continued unpacking her trunk, when one of the older African sisters came in.

"Dumayla, Mè." (Hello, Sister or madame)

"Dumayla," replied Johnna as she continued her unpacking.

The visitor picked up some Scotch tape and inquired what it was used for.

Johnna explained what it was used for, while she taped two pieces of paper to show her that it could hold them together.

"You give me?"

"Sure, take it," said Johnna feeling very generous.

In similar fashion, Johnna was relieved of a ruler, a red ballpoint pen, a set of colouring pencils and a three-ring hardcover binder. She was very generous in nature and would have given the shirt off her back as the saying goes. This would also lead to her downfall.

In the days that followed, Sister Inez, the superior cum principal began briefing the newcomers for their teaching assignments. She showed them their classes; gave them their list of duties for supervision, etc. She explained that the students arrived in January and stayed until June when they went home for a month's holidays. Then they came back in July and stayed until November when they wrote their final exams. She tried to explain the African curiosity for all things Western.

"They not only want to see what you have but the also want to have it. Already, Sister Jo-anna, you have given Sister Rita many things without permission and which as an African she does not have permission to have. You must not forget that they have also made a vow of poverty which may not be the same as yours. Please refrain from doing this in the future, Sister."

She continued her briefing by explaining the social differences and behaviours. The greatest glory for a native woman in third world cultures, is to bear children. That is why there are pregnancies as early as Grade Four, in the elementary school. Be vigilant. Avoid all familiarity with students or staff adding that they had to be "kept in their place."

Johnna interrupted Inez, "What do you mean by "Kept in their place?"

"Well Sister, the political situation here in South Africa is a system of separate development; the whites on one side and the non-whites or the blacks, Coloureds and Asians on the other. The students from South Africa must adhere to all the apartheid laws when they return to South Africa."

"But surely the Church must be against such discrimination. We must not lord it over the Africans as though we were created superior to them," Johnna said, "Remember what Christ himself said when he was asked if they should respect the leaders of the day? "Render unto Caesar that which is Caesar's," he told them. "We are in this country as aliens and we must respect their laws or go back to Canada."

Inez finished her session by saying that learning Sesotho was not a priority for us like it was for the nurses. We had to converse in English so that students and staff would learn English better. Learning Sesotho was not a luxury that we could afford.

Irene joined Johnna in her classroom afterwards where they shared their reactions.

"Gosh, Johnna, "the white sisters seem to stick together and the Africans form their own group. How are we to cope when Mooya tells us that we must keep our distance?"

"Well my dear, I'm just going to be myself and be true to myself as my father always taught me. I'll try to be honest with my reasons for being here and live up to my beliefs. The colonizers really thought they were bringing civilization to this part of the world and it was at the onset based on the Gospel. The Church now, is not speaking out against apartheid, claiming that it should not be political. I believe that they are taking the easier route out, which I do not agree with. I find that it contradicts the spirit of our Foundress, Mother Celeste, who said that our students must always be served by us, not the other way around. "We are to be the servants of the poor," she said; I guess I'm a bit of a radical but I agree with her."

"I feel the same as you do but I can't express it as succinctly."

"Remember the song, "I gotta be me. What else can I be? I gotta be me!" That's my theme song now," said Johnna.

# Chapter Eight

Johnna sang the words of her theme song softly as she worked away at her lesson preparations, "I gotta be me, whatever will be, I gotta be me." She was interrupted by the entry of a student.

"Dumela, Mè"

"Dumela. And who are you?"

"My name is Veronica Moshlana. I will be in J.C.1 this year."

"Welcome, Veronica. You speak English very well. Where are you from?"

"Thank you Mè. I am from Dube Township. That is pronounced Du-bay and it is in Soweto."

"Pardon my ignorance, but where is Soweto?"

"It is a black urban area outside of Johannesburg. It really means South Western Townships and includes about twenty-six separate towns of which Dube is one."

"I see," said Johnna as she wrote on the chalkboard, So-We-To. "This is what is called an acronym, which is a word that is formed from an initial or initial letters from other words. But how did you ever come to Basutoland to study?"

"I completed my Basutoland Primary Teachers' Certificate, which is called by the acronym, B.P.T.C.," She smiled proudly.

What a brilliant girl, thought Johnna. I wonder what Inez meant when she said that the Africans were dense and unteachable?

"I live with my elder brother Joseph and his family since my father was killed in a mining disaster in Benoni. My Mother died six years previously of childbirth complications. Bantu Education for blacks in the Townships is so watered down that when we complete Standard Six, which I learned is called Grade Eight in Canada, we are not accepted in regular Secondary Schools except the watered down ones for Africans in the townships. With these Bantu Secondary School Certificates we are not accepted for scholarships abroad. Because I had completed my B.P.T.C. I was accepted here where the course is not watered down. The Cambridge Overseas O-Level taught in Lesotho gives us the opportunity, if we are successful to study abroad. I will sit the exams in 3 years, and hopefully will get good enough marks to be accepted for a bursary at a university overseas."

"Well, we'll work very hard and hopefully you will succeed."

"Thank you, Mè. Please tell me where I will sit so I can put my books away."

"Right here in front of my desk, so that I can have moral support tomorrow when lessons begin!"

The next morning, there were six girls and two Sister-students when Inez introduced her to the class. At first Johnna felt very strange before this sea of various hues of brown faces. After a few short weeks however, Johnna never noticed their "blackness" but only saw persons with their individual characteristics and traits.

In her first letter to Mother Judith, the Superior General in Toronto, she wrote:

> *"... As I get to know the students more and more, they lose their blackness and become simply individuals. I have been warned by Sister Superior not to become too familiar with the students or with the African sisters. This advice, it seems to me, lumps the blacks as "them" and the whites as "us". No wonder she finds the Africans "dense and unteachable"! I am afraid, Reverend Mother, that I am unable to practice this "religious apartheid". As I see it in practice here, it creates two camps; one for the pro-Africans and one for the pro-whites. Among the pro-whites are the "chosen" Africans, who do the bidding of the whites who protect them. Conversely the pro-Africans are those who are not in the "inner circle". The lines of division are not along colour lines! I pray God that I will not be swayed by unhealthy allegiances, one way or the other."*

Johnna reread her letter and wondered what the effects of this "apartness" had on individuals, especially the Africans who didn't have a "free country" to return to, like the whites, known as Europeans in South Africa. She found out the next day after school when Veronica, who had been working at her desk, looked up at her and said,

"Mè, why am I the black one and you the white one?"

Johnna was taken aback by the question and hesitated. Silently she begged the Holy Spirit to inspire her with the correct answer.

"It's a universal question, Veronica, asked by the have-nots in a multitude of situations throughout the world. In my present situation, I have given up a comfortable life in Canada to live here in a Third World situation, to help the Basuto find a better life some day through education. I have freely chosen a more difficult life to accomplish this. This makes me a single "C", because I am here by Circumstances only. But no matter how sincere or trusting we Europeans are we are always separated by colour and culture. But you, you have all three "C's". You have the Circumstances, the Colour and the Culture. It's what I call "C Cube" or C to the third power. That translates into an influence that is three times stronger than mine could ever be. It's what the distinguished African poet, Leopold Senghor coined "la négritude", which he used first to express the Black African literary and artistic experience. Later, he used it to mean the political and economic issues. He wanted his fellow countrymen to "assimilate" which is to absorb information etc. into the mind and not be "assimilated" which is causing a weaker culture to acquire the characteristics of a stronger culture and thus lose itself. He is now the President of an Independent Senegal. He has accomplished much for his country because of his "Blackness". I hope that helps to explain why you are black and I am white. It's just an accident of birth that we must make the best of. We'll talk about this issue again later."

The weeks passed quickly and Johnna was continuously learning as she taught. The English course for the Junior Certificate covered three years. Within the three years, the students studied one novel, one Shakespearean play, selected poetry and mega doses of grammar. This year, 1960, was the first year that Saint Joseph Secondary School had begun. Before the finals in three years, the school was projected to have over 150 students. Johnna fondly called her class the "Pioneers" since they were the first graduates.

The novel that they were studying was "The Tale of Two Cities" by Charles Dickens. To Johnna's surprise, the passivity and seeming disinterest in class was not a measure of the absorption of the material. She was supervising the evening meal one day, when she overheard something surprising.

"Miss Manette, please bring some water for the wash-up!"

When the water was placed on the table, Francina said,

"There you are Madame LaFarge!"

Johnna surmised that the trim Francina was Miss Manette and Madame La Farge was the buxom Bernadette, who knitted all the time in actuality. Much to her delight, she realized that they had absorbed the true characters of the novel! As she made her supervisory rounds after clean-up, she came upon a row down by the latrines. Eva, a coloured girl from Bechuanaland, was vehemently arguing with some local Basuto girls. Johnna broke up the melee, took Eva aside and away from the other girls who continued to squabble in Sesotho.

"Now Eva, tell me what this is all about."

"Mè, they call me a Boer because my father is a Boer but my mother is Tsawana. I use her family name of Kukami because she never married the Baas. I am not a Boer!"

I must get someone to talk to those girls, thought Johnna. But who? Veronica is too soft spoken and because she is of the same tribe they will not listen to her.

Jeannette is far too overbearing and she'll just get their backs up. I need someone, of a different tribe who is strong and fair. Umm, I think Francina will do. She sent for Francina.

Francina Tsolo was a Xhosa from the Transkei. She was born in a small village called Libode near Umtata. Both of her parents were Xhosa although her paternal grandfather had been an Afrikaner storekeeper. She had hated him for marrying her paternal grandmother. This made her fiercely Xhosa and she used creams to darken her skin just as Eva used creams to lighten hers. She was tolerant and refused to treat people as inferior because they were not of her tribe. Yes thought Johnna, she had firmness and a sense of justice rare in a person her age and would make an excellent arbitrator. She called her over, explained the situation and asked her to speak to the girls in question.

"Speak to them in Sesotho. Tell them that they are practicing a subtle form of apartheid by discriminating against Eva."

"Mè, may I explain something to you first?"

"Of course Francina, by all means do."

"The girls who were arguing with Eva are not totally wrong. Eva was born in Ramotswe, Bechuanaland. Her father is a Boer rancher. He had an Afrikaner wife and eight children when he sired Eva by her mother who is the family cook. In 1950, when Eva was only thirteen she registered as White under the new Population Registration Act because she is obviously very pale and because she wants to be white! To help her in her dream, her mother sent her here to get a people's education."

"What is a people's education?"

"It is an alternative to the "Bantu Education" taught to Africans in South Africa; it is such a watered down programme that blacks cannot proceed to any other Secondary School other than a Bantu Secondary School, which is also watered down. This means that there is no chance to get a scholarship to go to the University or to study abroad. Her mother insisted that she come here even if she is classified as white on her documents. Eva also uses whitening creams and straightens her hair constantly with hot stones. So you see the girls are not totally wrong."

"Thank you for enlightening me, Francina, but still they should not abuse her."

"Eh Mè. I shall so advise them."

The first school year came to an end and Johnna was grateful for her time alone. She would catch up on her correspondence and do her long range plans for the next school year. As the bus climbed the hill to the main road, she heard the girls singing, "Kanete, kea mo rata! Kanete kea mo rata!" She remembered that Jeannette, with a strong voice sang, "Gosh, I love her! Gosh, I love her" at the farewell soiree a few days ago. She also remembered that Sister Inez had stared mercilessly at her when the girls showed her so much affection. A crisp voice broke her reverie,

"Sister Jo-anna, may I see you in my office, please."

"Yes, Sister Superior. Would you kindly call me by my name which is John-na?"

There was no apology. But Inez had her sit down once they were in the office.

"In a few days we will go to the Provincial House in Leribe for our annual retreat. There are some very serious faults that I have observed in you. I have itemized and documented all the incidents for you to ponder and pray over during those silent days. They all deal with "particular friendships" which you have created and continue to nurture in spite of my continued warnings. If you recall the first week that you were here, I told you to avoid familiarity with any particular students or staff. All the incidents that I have itemized deal with Sister Irene, Eva Kukami, Francina Tsola, and Veronica Mohlana to name a few. When you return from retreat we shall discuss this problem."

Johnna was sitting at her desk with her list in hand when Irene walked in and said,

"Did you get mail?"

"No. It's a list of incidents that Mooya has made, itemizing all my particular friendships. How did she get all these particulars? She must have spies everywhere!"

"Did she discuss them with you?"

"No, she wants me to meditate on them during retreat and discuss them with her when we return. She also wants to know if that picture of Alan at the prom is my brother. That can only mean that she has been through my trunk!"

Before leaving for retreat Johnna put all her personal pictures, letters and writings in a four gallon candy tin called a "billy can". She stored it the cupboard where the rats were said to be. Nobody ever opened that cupboard she had been told. Her privacy was assured.

# Chapter Nine

During the retreat, Johnna wrote a long letter to Mother Judith, It was the only way she had to vent her feelings and frustrations without being disloyal. She knew that Mother Judith would not only understand but also advise her.

>Dear Mother Judith,
>
>My first year is over! Here at retreat I can ponder over, review, and take firm resolutions to make 1961 a better year.
>
>Conflicts continue to arise with Sister Inez. She seems unable to listen or accept changes, which could better the plight of Africans especially the African Sisters. She uses double standards in her treatment of the latter. She has a contingent of them who act as her spies whom she rewards with candy when she returns from shopping in town. This causes much dissension among them, because those who do not receive sweets are jealous and rightly so.
>
>Sister Berthilde continues to badger me, because I teach in the Secondary School while she has been here almost ten years and is still teaching Standard VI. I try to explain to her that I didn't name myself to the job. When I spoke to Sister Superior about it, she said it couldn't be, because Sister makes her Stations of the Cross every day. Whatever that has to do with it?
>
>Sister Superior made me a list of incidents, highlighting what she calls my particular friendships with Sister Irene and three of my students. She has asked me to pray over them and we will discuss them when we are back at Saint Joseph's. Seriously, I don't think we will ever agree on much!
>
>The European Missionaries have social entrapments of their own. Their rationalization seems to excuse any moral implications. Some justify their own form of apartheid just as the Boers do. As though it were God who is responsible for the unequal distribution of grace! The categories used for their justifications are similar to that of the Boers; biological inheritance, blood, culture, background, education, mentality, and intelligence — you name it.

*While the White Missionaries live a life of ease and considerable luxury, the Tower of Babel rises higher and higher. Theirs is a policy of "constructive engagement" with their own particular sincerities, but without direct involvement. These individuals who enjoy the priviledge of power, are also paradoxically victims of it too! I want no part of it and am willing to pay the price! It pains me to no end that anyone who sincerely and honestly works to better the life of the Africans, is persecuted.*

*By my friendship with the Afrikaners and Africans alike, I am accumulating first-hand knowledge of the situation and will be better able to make a positive contribution. Is that not why we are here?*

*Yours in Christ,*
*Sister Johnna*

*P.S. I have learned that it is possible to have certain sympathy with people whose values one finds reprehensible. It is the only hope for a solution to the South African problem. Pray God that I may use this theory in my relationship with Sister Inez.*

After returning to Saint Joseph's, the new term preparations began immediately, the coil mattresses were shaken, the washstands painted, linoleum installed over the new mud floors in the classrooms and the dormitories, etc. Johnna waited with a certain apprehension for the call from Sister Inez to discuss the famous list, but it never came Johnna greeted her eight pupils for the 1961 school year, with her usual enthusiasm.

"Welcome to JC 2. Does anyone know what JC 2 means grammatically? Yes Suzanne."

"It's an abbreviation, Mè."

"Well, an abbreviation is a shortened or contracted form of a word or phrase. For example; Dr. for Doctor. An acronym on the other hand is formed from the initial letter of a series of words such as JC for Junior Certificate or Soweto for South Western Townships. So there is a difference between the two. Last year we studied a novel. Do you remember the title and the author, Miss Manette?"

When the laughter subsided, Francina said, "It was A Tale of Two Cities by Charles Dickens."

"Right," said Johnna, "this year we will study a play by William Shakespeare, an Englishman, who was one of the greatest writers in English history. Dickens, you remember lived in 1564 and died in 1616. What century was that, Eva?"

"Mè, it's two centuries, the 16$^{th}$ and 17$^{th}$."

"Correct. It was before the Industrial Revolution in England and the abolition of aristocracy and clerical priviledge in France, which brought about the French Revolution from 1789 to 1815. Also as Eva said it spanned two centuries. Shakespeare wrote during an agrarian and cottage industry economy, with the Tudor Kings as the rulers. He wrote a lot about the courts and the royals. Some of his plays were comedies, others were tragedies. We will start with a comedy because it is easier to understand. The one that I have chosen is the "The Merchant of Venice". Our Geography and History Courses are all about Southern Africa. You will help me with some of the pronunciations, I am sure. She tried to pronounce P-O-T-G-I-E-T-È-R-S-R-U-S as she wrote it on the board which is famous for producing tin. "They laughed at her pronunciation and repeated it for her to learn.

"The teachers of the other various subjects will explain their courses when you meet them. On your list are names of the texts you need and the teachers who teach each subject. The extra-curricular activities are new this year and are also listed with the staff members that will monitor them. I will be the monitor for the Geography-History Club and we will meet twice a week, Tuesdays and Thursdays after study until the generator goes off at nine-thirty. On the evenings that you have a club meeting, you must do your ablutions after supper and before study, so that when the lights go out you can just hop into bed. That will be all for today."

"Mè, when can we join the club?" asked Veronica.

"Anytime. Just go to the monitor and give your name to her."

"I want to join the Geography-History Club," said Veronica.

"Me too," said Francina.

"And me too," said Eva.

My my, thought Johnna, this should make Inez happy!

Just then Sister Emily appeared and asked to join the club.

"Of course, you are welcome," said Johnna.

Johnna supervised the study on the first evening, from seven to eight-thirty. As she sat there, she looked at her list of club members and began to write entries into her log book.

EVA KUKAMI: A coloured girl, ostracized by the others because she is coloured. Very pale and very pretty. Born in 1943 and is now 17 years old. Her father is an Afrikaner cattle rancher near Romotswe, Bechuanaland. She has eight white half-brothers and half-sisters by her father's Boer wife. He sired Eva with her mother who is the family cook. She is a Tswana and her name is Sekone Kukami. Eva used her mother's surname Kukami.

FRANCINA TSOLO: Is very pale but resents any implication of white blood. Is related to Nelson Mandela by blood and political allegiance as a member of the Youth Arm of the ANC (Whatever that acronym means). Born in Libode near Umtata in 1941, and is now 20 years old. Both parents are Xhosa but her paternal grandfather was an Afrikaner storekeeper. She was ashamed of her father's father and blocks out this part of her genealogy. She uses creams to darken her skin. (I know because she asked me to borrow my tanning lotion). She is intelligent and very beautiful.

VERONICA MOHLANA: Is a Mosuto, born in Soweto (Dube Town). Her father was killed in a mining accident in Benoni. Her mother died six years previously in childbirth. Her older brother, Joseph with whom she now lives, has a large family but recognizing Veronica's abilities, he has made many sacrifices to send her to BPTC in Basutoland. Now is paying for her Junior Certificate studies so that she may apply to study overseas. She is twenty-one years old.

SISTER EMILY: I don't know anything about her. Gee, I hope she isn't one of Inez's spies!

She left a space below each entry for future information as time went on. After study, she hid her club notebook in the billycan in the cupboard of her bedroom. She wore gloves to make sure that she left no trace on the door.

On Tuesday evening after study, the Geography-History Club had their first meeting. Johnna had done a lot of research and made a chart which she hoped to put up at each meeting. She began by saying that they should find a suitable name for their club, something shorter than Geography-History. Something catchy.

"Any ideas? asked Johnna as she further explained.

"We must sympathize with people whose values one finds evil or different. Otherwise how will we ever learn to trust each other enough to sit down and discuss our problems."

As each student gave her thought Johnna wrote them on the chalkboard.

| Quest | Q |
| Understand | U |
| Explore | E |
| Sympathize | S |
| Trust | T |

"I can't believe it!" exclaimed Johnna, "It forms the word, QUEST! We have formed a perfect acronym. Let's vote for this as our club name."

The vote was unanimous. Then Johnna put up the chart she had made and they all gasped.

"I won't bore you with details, because I have duplicated copies for each of you on the Gesterner when I went to the provincial house in Leribe yesterday, after lessons. Just let me say that 175 million years ago the earth's land mass was one huge continent called Pangaea. There were two bulges; Laurasia in the north and Gondwandaland in the south, from which Africa was formed three million years ago. You can read all that occurred from then until the Iron Age farmer came into contact with Europeans on the South African coast. Of particular interest to us, was Jan Van Riebeck's establishment of the Cape refreshment station for the Dutch East India Trading Company's ships. Our academic geography course begins there and ends with WWII. So we will deal with many aspects in class. Our club will explore South Africa from the war to the present by discussion, sharing, and research. We don't want any stories like the Boers grow good potatoes because their soil is fertilized with dead blacks. Remember, we must be truthful about our findings."

"One of our quests is to get information since the end of WWII, May 8th, 1945 to the present. We will cover such topics as White Politics, Resistance Politics, and Labour. Unrest as these relate to all South Africans. Each of us will contribute information about these three topics for Thursday's meeting, anything you can find. We need a secretary, who will write down all the information and organize our findings. I volunteer to type the notes for distribution. Is there someone who will volunteer for the post of secretary?

Veronica raised her hand.

# Chapter Ten

Early in January, 1962, classes began in earnest for the students of Saint Joseph's Secondary School at Khukhune, Basutoland. The school population had swelled to seventy-nine girls. The Hololo River had also swollen with the abundance of summer rains. The countryside was green; the gardens abundant with fruits and vegetables. Everything should have been right with the world!

Contrasting with this lush and generous harvest was the bourgeoning struggle for independence. Ghana was the first British Colony to become independent in March, 1957. Kwame Nkrumah became a model for all aspiring politicians in the British Colonies of Africa. The big giant, "African Continent" was straining to rise. Traditional African patrimonialism was dying a slow death.

The political picture in Basutoland was shared by three political parties. The Basutoland Congress Party, (BCP) established in 1952 and led by Ntsu Mokhehle. He had been educated at Fort Hare University before it was reduced to a Tribal Xhosa College in 1959. Chief Jonathan Leabua founded the Basutoland National Party (BNP) in 1958. The Marema Tlou Party (MTP) had been begun in 1957 to protect the monarchy of Basutoland.

On the first day of lessons, Bernadette, a.k.a. Madame LaFarge, asked Johnna, "When will the wedding take place?"

"Which wedding?"

"Yours Mè."

"Mine? What on earth are you talking about?"

"Didn't you hear the loudspeakers going by last night on the main road? Ntsu Mokhehle said that when he is elected Prime Minister, he will come and take you as his wife."

"How did you know that he meant me; there are twenty-three of us sisters here in the mission?"

"He mentioned the tall one with the satin dress."

"That is what is called propaganda, in this case an organized communist programme of publicity and selected information. Usually politicians use it to confuse the people. Believe me, if people think that I would agree to this, then that really will confuse them. They know that we do not marry. Ntsu knows that if he can confuse the people about us, then that will weaken our influence. One of the biggest stumbling block that we have in discovering the truth is misinformation."

Jeannette blurted out, "Mè, my uncle told me a story about Ntsu Mokhehle when I was home. Mokhehle was travelling to Maseru from Roma, when he stopped to talk with a group of children on the road. He gave them some bread to eat as he spoke to them. Then he asked if anyone knew the "Our Father." He chose one boy to recite it. Then he corrected him saying, "No, no. God didn't give you the bread, I did. So you must say, "Mokhehle, who art here… give us our daily bread, and when I am elected, I will.""

That's interesting, Jeannette, but I must put in a warning here. I will not allow politics, be they ever so current or volatile, to interrupt our lessons. We have a curriculum to follow and cannot afford to use our time for anything else but lessons. That is why we formed the Quest Club where these discussions can be carried on, is that understood?"

Johnna wasn't sure if the silence that followed was understanding or the usual passivity when a black person is addressed by a white person. No matter, she continued her lesson.

"We will begin our study of literature this year by taking a look at some African writers, then selecting one piece to study in detail. Last year, we studied some of Léopold Senghor's poetry. He became the President of Sénégal in 1960. He wrote about "la négritude", which was a protest against French rule and the policy of assimilation. He looked at Western values in order to redevelop a pride in African culture. He attacked the soulessness of Western civilization. Do you remember the piece in which he wrote, "… no mother's milk, but only nylon legs, as a description of the women in our Western Culture?" Also he wrote, "We are the leaven that the white flour needs.""

"Now the poet we will study this year is Dennis Brutus, who wrote about the suffering of his fellow South African blacks under apartheid. He was born of South African parents in Rhodesia in 1924. He graduated from the only university in South Africa for blacks, called Fort Hare. He has been teaching in a Secondary School since 1948. His poetry is beautifully crafted and reflects his struggle for justice. His outspoken protests against social discrimination in sport got him an 18-month prison sentence. He was also banned from teaching, writing, publishing, attending social or political meetings and from pursuing studies in law at the Witwatersrand University. The selection I have chosen to study this year is called, "Somehow We Survive."

Johnna wrote the poem on the chalkboard for the students to copy. She wrote:

> "Somehow we survive
> and tenderness, frustrated, does not wither.
> Investigating searchlights rake
> our naked unprotected contours;
> over our heads the monolithic Decalogue
> of fascist prohibition glowers and teeters
> for a catastrophic fall;
> boots club at the peeling doors.
> But somehow we survive
> severance, deprivation, loss.
> Patrols uncoil along the asphalt dark
> hissing their menace to our lives,
> most cruel, all our land is scarred with terror,
> rendered unlovely and unlovable;
> sundered are we and all our passionate surrender
> but somehow tenderness survives".
> –Dennis Brutus.

When they had copied the poem, they looked up all the words they didn't know in their dictionaries. For one week, they discussed the passage and memorized it.

At the meeting of the Quest Club, Francina said, "Mè, I made a chart for our club."

She raised it for all to see. Johnna took it and placed it above the door of her bedroom and stood back as she read it.

> "Somehow we survive
> and tenderness, frustrated, does not wither
> …But somehow we survive
> severance, deprivation, loss.
> …'But somehow tenderness survives.'
> –Dennis Brutus.

There was a stunned silence in the group. Everyone felt the great emotion of the passage grip them. Johnna broke the spell.

"I will make the presentation tonight, so that at our next meeting one of you can make your own and we can begin discussions."

### **History Chart – JC II**

**AD**  1600— Iron Age farmers come into contact with the Europeans for the first time on the South East African coast.
1652—Cape refreshment station established by the Dutch East
India Company by Jan Van Riebeck. He imported Malay
and West African slaves for his plantations, since no blacks were indigenous to this region.
1750—Boers begin moving inland which leads to a decline in local Hottentots (known as Koikoi) who were mixed Bushmen (San) and Bantu and the appearance of the Cape Colored (of Boers and Hottentots parentage)
1795—First British occupation begins.
1800—Boers meet the Bantu Xhosa at the Fish River.
1806—British seize the Cape; Mfecane (Tribal Wars). This paved
the way for a policy and ideology of segregation; the allocation of reserve lands for Africans governed by traditional authorities; and the attempt to prevent African urbanization through a system of daily registered labour.

When each girl had a chart, Johnna continued her explanations.

"The "White problem" of South Africa began in 1652, when the Dutch East India Company sent Jan Van Riebeck and a group of company employees to the Cape of Good Hope, to establish a refreshment station for vessels travelling to the Indies. After a few years the Company allowed some of the employees to settle as "free burghers". This was the beginning of the two most important facts that set the stage for South Africa's history of segregation. First was the slavery and the second was the "trekking".

"The company imported the first shipload of slaves from Madagascar, Mozambique and the East Indies to the colony in 1658 and miscegenation began to flourish."

"Mè, Mè?" Francina interrupted, "What is that word Miss Cegenation? And what does it mean?"

In spite of herself Johnna blushed and said as she wrote the word on the board, "It means marriage between whites and blacks in South Africa. But it could also mean interbreeding of other races."

Johnna continued, "The first British occupation began in 1795 and they established themselves in charge in 1803. British immigration—the coming of British permanent settlers, with the support of the London Missionary Society helped to spread Christianity among the Africans. The Calvinist faith of the Dutch settlers helped to increase race consciousness and led to the belief that all dark-skinned people were the Biblical children of Ham, who was cursed by Noah and they were heathens or pagans."

"In time, the Western Cape became later known as the Coloured District. The sedentary free burghers employed Coloureds on their farms and they produced wine, fruit and wheat."

"Other free burghers began to travel north in search of land for their cattle and sheep. These supplied the meat needs of Cape Town. The poor pastures however, were quickly depleted and so the Dutch settlers now known as Boers, trekked further and further into the interior. They met and warred with the Hottentots from 1659 to 1673. As they advanced they met the various Bantu tribes and these wars became known as the "Kaffir Wars" from 1779 to 1850. The Boers were too poor to buy slaves, so they made slaves of the Kaffirs and the Basuto who were destitute after the wars.

"Between 1846 and 1864, about one-sixth of the colony was set aside solely for Africans. Since there was plenty of land, the Africans saw no need to work for the settler farmers. This caused them to be taxed with such levies as the hut tax. It also explains why indentured labour contracts with the government of India, recruited Indian workers for sugar plantations in Natal province."

"Mè," Eva asked, "Do we have to remember all that you talked about today?"

"No, no! Of course not. I've given you all the notes in print. We will take all year to study, understand, discuss and memorize each section. But today I have given you an "overview" of the whole year's course. Does that answer your question?"

"Eh Mè! Thank you."

"In the 1830's the Boer Voortrekkers, organized a migration north and east to escape British rule. The British left them alone to clear the land and fight the various tribes from whom they took the land by devious arrangements with the chiefs."

"The discovery of diamonds near the present day Kimberley in 1867 and gold in 1871, brought the British rushing back to lay claim to the lands. The British and the Boers fought several battles against each other. The Boers defeated the British at Majuba, but in the end the British defeated the Boers in the famous Boer War at the turn of the century."

"The Union of South Africa came into being in 1910, with Louis Botha as Prime Minister. In 1913, General J.B.M.Hertzog formed a new "purified" National Party and white rule became enshrined in parliament. Between 1913 and 1936, the reserve African lands had been reduced to 13 per cent from 33 percent by the Native Lands Acts and the Whites now occupied 87 per cent of the land. In 1923, the Natives (Urban Areas) Act extended segregation to the towns. In 1925, Afrikaans became the second official language. In 1927, 64 new "locations" were established for Africans outside urban areas.

Johnna had been so involved in all her lesson preparations and Quest Club research that she did not notice the storm heading her way. Nor did she realize that Inez was the eye of the storm! She got the first hint of trouble brewing when Irene said that the Bishop was coming to Khukhune, but not in an official capacity.

"And just what does that mean?" queried Johnna.

"Well, some of the African sisters said that he was very upset at what was going on at the school."

"What is going on at the school that I don't know about?"

"Sister Lucia told me that the Bishop was upset with you."

"Me? Whatever for?"

"She said that you are spreading civil discontent among the students by teaching them that the government of South Africa is evil. You also have criticized the Church's position on the apartheid issue."

"I have only spoken the truth, Renie. There are 77 per cent of South Africans that identify themselves as Christian. But there are Christians on both sides of the apartheid conflict. Do the Africans share a creator God with white South Africans who are a source of generations of misery to the Africans? Is it, "My God, our God, and their God?" I am only sharing the light of the reality of the situation so these girls will help to rehumanize their people. Surely it is the same God who created to His own image all human beings, of all races, languages and countries."

"Hey, Johnna, I am not your enemy! I'm your pal, remember? I'm only telling you what I heard."

"Thanks, Renie. That gives me time to prepare my defence."

At three o'clock, Johnna went to the dining room for tea and Inez approached her with, "Sister Joanna, will you please accompany me to the rectory?"

That didn't take long, thought Johnna. Walking behind the silent Inez, she thought of the condemned persons being conveyed in a tumbrel to their execution during the French Revolution. She wondered if the Bishop would give her the guillotine?

After the usual greeting ritual and without preamble the Bishop began.

"Sister Johnna, I am afraid that I have heard very disturbing news about your activities here in the school. Your superiors have sent you to teach the curriculum and not to do politics. The Church has remained neutral with regard to the conflict in South Africa. The Church feels that we are missionaries to the Africans. We are allowed to remain here only because of the tolerance of the government. If we upset the apple-cart we may well find our efforts curtailed. We must respect the powers that be or return to our homelands. Do you understand, sister?"

"Yes, your excellency."

Johnna had refrained from answering because she felt that it would only fall on deaf ears. She was sure that Inez expected an outburst of self-defence similar to the one that occurred when she had spoken to Johnna herself. Johnna had learned to curtail her enthusiasm.

Renie was waiting for her back in her class but Johnna felt a need to go over what had happened in the silence of her heart. Johnna's only safety valve was a letter to Mother Judith, the Superior General, which she set to immediately.

> *Dear Mother Judith,*
>
> *I am not preaching the gospel per se, but surely I must be here in the name of the gospel? An incident occurred which made me wonder. I rode the tumbrel and expected the guillotine to come crashing down when I appeared before the Bishop of Leribe today!*
>
> *I have been asked not to "do politics" as he put it. He said that I had been sent here to teach the curriculum and be a representative of Jesus Christ. He also said that if we don't respect the powers that be, we should return to our homelands. You would have been proud of me because I didn't even try to defend my position. But I can share my feelings with you.*
>
> *How can I be representing Jesus Christ if I cannot preach the gospel? Because the gospel in South Africa is closely bound up with social, political and economic history. The gospel of the Dutch and the British justified and legitimized colonialism, imperialism and European superiority. In spite of using barbaric methods and attitudes, the colonizers really believed that what they were bringing here was a civilization rooted on the message of Jesus Christ. Neither the British nor the Boers doubted that God was on their side. They established the settler Church for the whites and the missionary Church for the Africans. Out of the missionary Church some prophetic figures appeared and from the associations a voice of prophecy is being heard. Both reject the evil of apartheid. What is preached is not always prophetic and I feel that my students have a right to be enlightened.*
>
> *Mother, I cannot bury my head in the sand when it comes to giving my girls all that I can to prepare them for the difficult life they have ahead. I want you to know that if you sincerely think*

*that it would be in their better interest and for their good that I return to Canada, feel free to recall me at any time.*

*Yours in Christ.*
*Johnna*

Johnna and Renie went for a walk after supper. Down the hill across the donga and up the hill to the village. Tom, the bus driver who daily went into Leribe, lived there. When he saw the sisters he greeted them warmly.

Johnna took out a pair of men's trousers that her mom had sent for the poor and offering them to him said, "Tom, this letter must be posted to my paramount chief in Canada. Could you do that for me tomorrow?"

"Eh Mè."

# Chapter Eleven

Johnna sat at her desk in the small classroom adjacent to her bedroom. It has been the former rectory before the present priest designed a native-styled rondovel for his lodgings. Her six girls and two native Sisters made up the first graduates of Saint Joseph's Secondary School. At the end of 1962, this group would sit their Cambridge Overseas "O Level" exams, sent out from London, England. Success in these exams would make it possible for them to enter post-secondary schools outside of South Africa. Especially good results could help them obtain bursaries overseas in English speaking countries. She had some brilliant girls in her class and it was imperative to prepare them for success.

She had spent all of last year dealing with the history of South Africa from 1600 to 1946 after World War II. She covered the politics of Basutoland itself but did not involve them in any partisan discussions.

Johnna, one day suggested that the Quest group prepare to present highlights of that time-span, from 1946 to the present, to the staff and other students. They could use any method of presentation as long as there were notes to hand out to all the Form III students for study purposes. They would cancel the Quest Club meetings for two weeks to give them time to prepare.

During that time she noticed a lot of activity that included many of the Form I and Form II girls.

The day for the resumption of the club meeting was on schedule. Veronica, as president of the group gave a few introductory explanations.

"Just a few words, since some of the Makhoa (Europeans or whites) who are attending tonight's presentation have recently arrived in Basutoland, may not know or understand the terms used in our play. I will give a short explanation before the play begins." She proceeds,

"In South Africa, according to the National Party which holds the power, there are two groups of people; the whites or "Blanke" and the "Nie-Blanke" who are all the other non-whites whom they call by the derogatory name of "Kaffir". The whites, since the rise of Communism in various countries of Africa became obsessed with "separate" public facilities. Everywhere in public buildings, on trains and buses, at airports and railway stations, at race courses and sports grounds, in restaurants, hotels, cinemas and theatres, on beaches and in graveyards, the non-white population was forced into separate areas. Needless to say the non-white areas were neglected and sub-standard! Signs were posted everywhere: "Blanke" or "Nie-Blanke"; on park benches, elevators, libraries, liquor stores and taxis. To keep non-whites as inferiors many laws and regulations were employed by the government controlling every aspect of their existence such as employment and residence; where they could or could not live. They even controlled the movements of the blacks. No section of the population was left untouched. No fewer than 231 different measures were employed by the creators of apartheid, as the separateness became known as. At every turn, the non-white population endured greater restrictions and greater hardships."

"The First Act of our play is about "White Politics and the Population Registration Act of 1950" by the then ruling National Party led by Dr. D. F. Malan. The whites, known locally as Afrikaners or Boers, formed a secret society called the "Broederbond" in 1918, with a view to controlling areas of government such as Afrikans culture, finance, and industry. Afrikaners were called "De Volk" and they believed that they had been chosen by God to subjugate all the other tribes in His Name." Veronica thanked the audience.

On a large chart on the chalkboard they had printed:

**"A Play in Three Acts"**

**South Africa — 1946 to 1962**

By the Quest Club.

Veronica gave the actors a few minutes to place themselves before she held up a small chart which read,

"Act I — White Politics and the Population Registration Act of 1950

## SCENE 1 — A Broederbond Meeting

### Dr. D.F.Malan  [Eva Kukami]
"The national Party came to power in 1948 because DeVolk wanted racial apartheid as our party adopted. They wanted blood purity. It is our ethnic identity as a people chosen by God!"

### Brothers of the Broederbond (Form I students) Shouting….
"Baaskop! Mastership! Domination!"

### Dr. D.F. Malan
"Godless Communism is a modern devil that we must fear. So in 1950 we legislated the "Suppression of Communism Act" to slay the demon."

### Brothers
""Grand apartheid!" "Grand apartheid!"

### Dr. D.F. Malan
"The natives must not be urbanized. We must develop homelands around where they were born, so that they can become independent. The native Influx Control Act restricts their movement into our areas. We will thus purify our towns!"

### Brothers
"Basskop! Basskop!" (Master over his servant)

> Johnna clapped and clapped as the group went into the hall.
> Veronica continued by holding the next chart.

## SCENE 2 — "A Police Arrest"

### Policeman — (Francina)
"You man. You are of the Herrenvolk. (Master race). You should realize that living with a Kaffir is restricted by the 1949 Mixed Marriage Act."

**Afrikaner: — (Eva)**
"Ag, meneer (sir). I love her and she bore my child. Let me stay with her."
**Policeman** "No Bladdy way! You are both off to jail!"
While the cast prepares again, Veronica holds the chart up.

## SCENE 3 — 1953
### A coloured girl is picked up in a bordello.

**Magistrate: — (Francina)**
"What is your name?"
**Coloured girl: — (Eva)**
"My name is Tandia."
**Magistrate:**
"Where do you live?"
**Coloured girl:**
"In Soweto."
**Magistrate:**
"Show me your identification papers."
[She hands him her papers which he carefully studies.]
"You were caught in prostitution with a white man. You contravened the Immorality Act of 1950. According to the Groups Areas Act, also of 1950, you are endorsed back to your village of Tamachu the Ciskei."

The narrator explains that in 1953, Hendrik Verwoerd, the then Minister of Education, passed the Bantu Education Act which established separate schools for Coloureds, Indians and blacks. The latter, were developed along tribal lines. In 1954 a Resettlement Act permitted the wholesale razing of the squatter towns, older mixed neighbourhoods, and forced relocation of their mixed populations into new government housing schemes like in Soweto, which were also subdivided on racial and tribal lines. In 1956, the Industrial Conciliation Act created the awkward multi-tiered system for regulating the industrial labour relations. Basically this restricted blacks from striking and kept them from jobs reserved for whites.

"We found these issues in Act II far too difficult to act out. Our last act has only one scene," She concluded.

## "Act 3 — Resistance
## "Finale"

**Cell Leader:** "Since the Treason Trial of the 156 activists in 1960, the arrest of Sobukwe for the Anti-Pass campaign and the Sharpeville shootings, which killed 67 and wounded 186 blacks, we have had to go further underground. Our reply to white terrorism and militarism—is war—the revolutionary war of liberation."

**Cell members:** "Freedom in our lifetime!" They shouted.

**Cell Leader:** "We are the Umkhonto We Sizwe—the spear of the Nation; Military wing of the African Nationalist Congress (ANC). We have always avoided violence but the laws get harsher and harsher until this year, Mandela announced that we must submit or fight. Poqo, the armed wing of the Pan African Congress Communist Party, has been very involved in sabotage. Now Madiba Intonga, our Black Pimpernel, as Mandela is also known orders us to speed up our sabotage. We will strike ISCOR, the iron and steel industry. And after that, SASOL, where petroleum is manufactured from coal. You have been given your marching orders. Ladies and gentlemen good luck."

**Cell Members:** "Mayi buye i Africa" (Let Africa return)

All the actors came out dancing the Kwela music to the rhythm of a penny whistle.

Johnna was deeply touched by the performance and she gave them a standing ovation. She thanked them profusely and then told them they had better rush to the dormitories because there were only three minutes to lights out.

# Chapter Twelve

"I called for you, Sister Johnna, because I hear that you are continuing to foment discontent among the Africans."

She must have really prepared her speech; she actually, for the first time in almost three years, called me by my real name, thought Johnna.

"You are advocating a rebellion against the Church and you are giving these girls false hope," continued lnez. "They will always be African and they must take their place in an apartheid society."

"I can't believe what I am hearing! In 1957, the Catholic Bishops of South Africa, declared that "apartheid is intrinsically evil". African Christians should not have to accept Western customs in order to be real Christians. Our students have to understand the gospel in terms of their black experience of suffering, humiliation, insecurity and oppression. You said that I am fomenting discontent and advocating rebellion against the Church? The simple fact is that the gospel in South Africa is associated with a political system that is now regarded by almost the whole world as a crime against humanity. If the hierarchy of the Church continues to use the gospel to avoid the present situation in South Africa, by arguing that this crime against humanity has nothing to do with God or salvation, then yes, I rebel against it! For a long time the people of South Africa listened and tried to make sense of this. But the youth in the townships have lost faith with all these confusing interpretations of the gospel. They are leaving the Church in the thousands, to them the Church is an obstacle to liberation and peace.

"Sister you are on the verge of heresy. We must save the gospel at all costs."

"The gospel doesn't need saving; it's the people that need saving.. All I am doing with my students, is trying to make the gospel relevant for their lives today. The truth shall make them free. I am only showing them the truth."

"Sister, this personal crusade of yours seems to describe the gospel as anything anyone wants it to mean. It has always been the tradition of the Church not to have the gospel open to any other interpretation but that of the magisterium. This is where you are approaching heresy."

"The gospel has always been contextual. It is not the letter of the law but the spirit that counts. The gospel has always meant good news. It is good news if it has a good effect on us. You say I have criticized the Church? I have criticized the fence sitting. I have criticized the leaders who betray the gospel. Preaching a gospel that tries to remain neutral with regard to the issues that adversely and deeply affect the lives of people, is in fact taking sides against them."

"You are opening a pandora's box with your new interpretations."

"If I am, so be it! But being new is not radical to the gospel. The word "new" was continually used in the Bible; a new song, a new heart, a new spirit, a new person, a new life, a new creation, a new covenant, a new age, new wine in new wineskins etc. The gospel can only be the same as in the past if it continues to be about the new things that God is doing today."

"Sister, I am afraid your ideas are too controversial. What you call reading the sign of the times with regards to South Africa is really just the gospel according to Sister Johnna!"

Inez continued, "The Bishop has recommended that you return to Canada at the end of the school year. The authorities in Toronto have been so advised."

Johnna welled up with indignation. She knew that it was all Inez' doing. Her jealousy at Johnna's successes had been noted over the years. Johnna felt that she had nothing to lose, so she blurted out.

"History repeats itself! In Jesus' times, He had observed the bankruptcy and hypocrisy of the religious establishment. I know that I have always been a thorn in your side. I'm sure you are well intended. But I am also aware that the devil uses good intentions to prevent the good from being done. What you call heresy, I call insight. This is what I have given the girls and it will live on long after I am gone. No one can take that away from me."

At the final meeting of the QUEST, Johnna told the girls that she would be returning to Canada soon after the closing of school. She explained to them that the authorities felt threatened by her ideas of helping the Africans. Johnna gave them her Mom's address and each ten Rand to buy stamps to write to her. She explained that the money was from the sale of the clothes her mother had sent for the needy.

The day before the students' departure there was a get-together in honour of the graduates. They sang a special song for Johnna called, "Kanete, kea mo rata" [Really, I love her] as Inez sat tight-lipped and unsmiling.

That evening at the final meeting of the QUEST Club, emotions ran high.

Johana said, "The Sotho name that the African sisters call me by is Pompanyane. It isn't very flattering; it means sick eyes. I understand that Africans feel that blue eyes are sickly and Pompanyane is that gunk that collects in the corner of sick eyes. But what Sotho name have you given me?"

There was a shuffling of feet and the girls looked at each other unwilling to divulge this secret.

"I know that Veronica's name is MaPaseka because she was born on Easter, so she is the Mother of Easter. But what name have you given me?"

"When you first arrived here in 1960, we were stunned at how pretty you were, especially with that swish-swish satin dress, so we called you Seponono and it means the "Pretty one", said Francina.

Blushing, Johnna asked, "And what is yours Francina?.

"MaMofirifiri" exclaimed Eva. "It means the Mother of Troubles because she is quick tempered and aggressive."

Francina jumped at the opportunity to retaliate against Eva. "They call her MaDithaba, which means the Mother of Dreams because she dreams of living in the white man's world some day."

They gathered around the globe and holding hands, recited:

"Somehow we survive.
and tenderness, frustrated does not wither.
…But somehow we survive
severance, deprivation, loss.…
But somehow tenderness survives."

# Chapter Thirteen

Early in 1963, Johnna found herself in Mother Judith's office once more. Johnna noticed how aged and ill she looked, but she was ever the same alert and vibrant friend.

"I am sorry to hear that you wish to leave the order, but I understand your reasons. I was afraid that it was bitterness that brought you to this decision."

"No, I have no bitterness; only gratitude to you for having given me that opportunity. It has helped me to see myself as I really am."

"When I sent you off to Basutoland, I thought I had made an error in judgment. I knew that you were outspoken and impetuous. I realized that you were an idealist but I also knew that you had a very generous nature and that you would weather anything to cling to your ideals. What I didn't know however, was just how deep the jealousy mounted against you would become. I had hoped that you could have changed our collective image in the mission field."

"How can that image be changed when all the eight Canadian congregations working there are the same? The Fathers and even the Bishop lead a life of priviledge. They have accepted apartheid because they are not victims of it."

"Yes, I have visited our missions there and the African sisters made me aware of the indifference of the Europeans to the suffering of their people and the realistic situation that they live in. The authorities to whom I have spoken of this dichotomy, tell me that it is not truthful because every one of them have had a higher standard of living in the order than they would have had at home."

"The African sisters are not complaining about their situation but that of their people. They feel that they should be allowed to go into the townships where they are really needed rather than live this life which to them is selfish and sterile."

"The African sisters have also written to me to express their sorrow at your untimely departure. They say that you were surely ahead of your times and that you had sincere empathy for their people. They have asked me to send you back."

"That's a comfort. They never told me that because they are afraid of any repercussions, if they go against the status quo. I certainly had no idea that they felt that way."

"I wish that I could promise to send you back someday but I may not be in this position for long. You know that there can be no such assurances in the religious life."

"Thank you for your continued support and understanding. I really appreciate it. I am leaving the order because I feel that it has strayed from its original mandate both at home and abroad—to relieve that plight of the poor. That was the spirit of the Foundress, Mother Celeste. That was what attracted me to the order in the first place. I feel that it has gone off on a tangent and will die out before it has a chance to go full circle. It has lost its "raison d'être". I only have one life to give to the poor. The Holy Spirit Missionaries do not fulfill my aspirations as I had hoped."

"It grieves me that it has come to this."

"Do not grieve Mother. I have learned so much. I always thought of poverty and suffering in an abstract manner. But I have seen the suffering of the Africans who witness their children dying of starvation. I have met people who have suffered at the mercy of cruel, insensitive torturers. What theologian Schillebeeck calls, "the barbarous excess of suffering." Being exposed to real suffering changes one forever. I also suffer from the Missionary Church's insensitivity to the suffering of those they go to serve. The ivory tower insensivity. They are totally unaware of the humiliation that is legalized in South Africa. Social engineering there, is all-pervasive and unjust. I acknowledged my responsibility as a priviledged white and contradicted the passive role taken by the Missionary Church. For that reason I was sent back to Canada."

"But you needn't leave the order. There is so much you can do here."

"Anyone who has been to Africa is compelled to return. It lays hold of your very soul."

Johnna stayed with Luke and his family in Willowdale, north of Toronto, for a few months when she first left the order.

"Are you going to find a teaching job?" Luke asked her one day.

"I don't think so, Luke. There's a course being offered for older women who want to get into nursing. It's called "Quo Vadis". It's a two-year course leading to an R.N. certificate. I want to take that and return to Africa."

"Why don't you get into the Foreign Service? You would have a more comfortable and secure life. You would be taken care of and have some security to come home to eventually."

Luke had become a veterinarian and had joined a lucrative practice in Toronto's Willowdale where he lived. He had married into a moneyed family. His two daughters attended Morrow Park in Willowdale, an elitist school run by the Sisters of Saint Joseph. What could he understand of Johnna's aspirations?

"Look Luke, just let me stay with you until I get settled. When I get everything in order, I'll be going out to Mom's in Souris, okay?"

"Sure, Sis. You can stay here as long as you wish. We are having a dinner party on Friday evening. Will you attend?"

"All right. As long as I am not too plain Jane for your crowd?"

"Never," he said.

By Friday, Johnna had applied and been accepted for the course. She had her train ticket to Brandon, where she had arranged for Matthew to pick her up to take her to her Mom's, who still lived on the family ranch. Slowly, slowly, she was beginning to unwind.

Soon it was Friday. The guests began to arrive for dinner. Johnna felt like an outsider; the only time anyone spoke to her was to ask disinterestedly about Africa. Then she noticed the back of a man's head and her heart beat fiercely. It couldn't be she thought. Just then Luke pointed her way and the man turned and stared. He approached her.

"Hello Johnna," he said.

"Why Alan... Luke didn't tell me..."

"He didn't tell me either, the fox."

Luke's complacent smile only accented his obvious delight. They spent the rest of the evening together, dancing, chatting and obviously happy to be reunited. Johnna spoke of her ambitions and dreams for the future. Alan listened patiently, then said:

"I haven't been with another woman intimately since you. I am still waiting for you. I love you Johnna. Will you marry me now?"

"Oh Alan. I love you too but I can't settle down yet. I promise you again that there will be no other man."

He kissed her then and when he got carried away, she broke it off saying, "Let's not make it too difficult for each other."

They said good night, promising to keep in touch.

On the train trip to Brandon, she thought of her mom. She knew that she would be very disappointed at her leaving the order, but hoped that she would understand why. If she did, it would help her to understand what was driving her back to Africa.

Matthew was at the station. He was still tall and handsome she thought and didn't look his thirty-seven years. He was the father of four now and by all accounts his children were bright and full of life.

"Hi, Sis. How are you?"

"I'm fine," she said as they hugged.

"You look thin and peaked to me. I hope you'll settle down now and we can get to know you again."

"I've been settled a long time but just not the way Dad had hoped. How's Mom?"

"She's aged since Dad passed away. The only time she looks perky is when she sees the kids. They bring out the spark in her."

"How did she take my leaving the order'?"

"She never talked about it at all."

Her mom had aged but Johnna thought she looked good. Over the few weeks, she and Johnna spoke more of the past than of the present. She avoided the future.

"Mom, can you understand why I left the order?"

"That's your business, Johnna. I do hope you'll settle down now."

Johnna said angrily: "What's with everybody? Is the only settling down as you call it, getting married and having kids?"

"No need to get angry, dear. We only want you to be happy."

"But I am happy. Just because my life is different it doesn't make me unhappy. The life I choose fulfills my needs and that makes me happy."

It was difficult leaving her mom this time. There was a feeling of finality in that last embrace.

"Follow your dreams, Johnna darling. I am always proud of you. I understand your dreams more than you think. My love and prayers are with you wherever you go."

"Thanks Mom. I count on that. I needed that. I love you very much too."

The nursing course was intensive and the two years sped by. In the last month before graduation she had met a missioner from Zambia. He had put her in touch with the Good Shepherd Sisters who ran a hospital at Mbala in the Northern Province of Zambia. They sent her application forms to be completed and assured her that air tickets would be sent for her travel to the mission. The contract was with the Catholic Secretariat in Lusaka which would pay her a salary, as well as air fare to and from Canada.

Johnna called Mother Judith to share her good news only to hear that she had passed away and been buried six months before.

"Would you like to speak to the new Mother General, Sister Caroline," asked the secretary.

"No. No thank you."

She put down the phone and had two reactions, She cried, because with Judith's passing part of her world fell out. Then she laughed and thought, "Am I glad I'm out of there! Yes!"

# Chapter Fourteen

It was the end of October 1967, when the Zambian Airway's plane brought Johnna to her second African experience. As the old dilapidated plane made its long, slow descent for landing, the door to the cockpit kept flapping open, making a bang every time it hit the opposite wall. Johnna sat in an aisle seat and when the door opened she could see the grassy parklands, dotted with small grass hut villages. Interspersed between the villages were large doughnut-like clearings. In the centre of some, she saw cut trees and branches piled high; in others she noticed smoldering mounds of ashes.

"What are those round clearings in the landscape?" Johnna asked the Zambian stewardess.

"Those circles are a method of traditional farming practiced by the Bemba tribe of Northern Zambia. It is called, "chitemene." Large circles are cut out of the forest. The branches and shrubs are burned and used as ash to fertilize their crops."

"What crops do they grow?"

"They produce maize, sorghum, millet and beans," the stewardess answered.

Soon the plane landed at the Lusaka International Airport. The welcoming party, consisted of two nuns and a middle-aged woman.

"Welcome, Johnna, I am Sister Bridget, the superior at Mbala. This is Sister Ellen, the matron at the hospital and Doctor Marguerite De Meus, a lay-missioner working at our station.

As Johnna shook hands with them, she asked,

"How did you recognize me? You didn't have to go through all this trouble."

"Well," said Ellen, "Father Bouchard wrote from Toronto and gave us a short description. You were the only white woman on the flight! Besides, we are always happy to shop in Lusaka."

"We will spend three days here before heading home to Mbala. We have to get home before the rains start, otherwise the unpaved roads become impossible. The road to Kasama is a "washboard" at the best of times but with the tropical storms, which come from November to February, our vehicle goes sideways in the deep ruts. Travellers have been caught for a few days in severe storms. We must get your work permit and contract signed before we head north. We will all stay at the Mission where the meals and accommodations are a reasonable price. The Fathers have built the Rest House to accommodate the outlying missioners."

In the evening, Johnna and Marguerite chatted in their room.

"You don't recognize me, do you?" queried Marguerite.

"Should I? I've never been to Zambia before?"

"I met you in Basutoland, South Africa in December 1962 when I fled from the Belgian Congo. My brother was a missionary priest working in Basutoland at the time. I went to him because I needed money to travel back to Belgium. Do you remember? I was still a sister then."

"Yes, now I remember. You look so different out of the habit!"

"So do you, Johnna, I recognized your name when the sisters said you were coming to work at the hospital. So I asked if I could come out to greet you. And here I am! But I thought you were a teacher. You seemed so happy and the students really appreciated you."

"That was part of the problem; they appreciated me too much! Vindicative jealousies arose and of course my views were not understood or appreciated. I thought the Church and the European missionaries were too impassive against apartheid. Most of them enjoyed a more comfortable life than they would have had in Canada. So the Bishop wanted to silence me because I was rocking the boat, so he had me recalled to Canada."

"I left my own congregation for similar reasons although I was expelled for political as well as moral reasons. The gutless Belgians and other Europeans had a great contempt for the locals ever since King Leopold II's exploitations with Stanley in the 1880's. They feared the natives and encouraged tribal rivalries and internecine struggles using the hostilities to their financial advantage. In 1960, at Independence, many colonial institutions and expatriate personnel were still in place and still harboured the same disdain. Congolese soldiers rebelled against their Belgian superiors. This led to civil war. Katanga Province rich in copper, cobalt, and uranium tried to secede under Moïse Tsombe. Belgian troops intervened and massacred many Africans. The Congolese rebels, in revenge, dressed in monkey skins and doped-up on amphetamines like African weed called "mira", they threatened to cut out the hearts of thirteen hundred white hostages in Stanleyville and dress themselves in their flayed skins."

"It must have been so frightening!"

"Yes. One night, at our mission hospital near the river port of Basoko, we heard very strange whistling noises different from the usual forest noises that we had grown accustomed to. The African sisters knew instinctively that the rebel Simbas were on a spree and fearing rape were ready to take their chances and flee into the forest. That was when I got the brainwave that became our salvation. Our hospital was on an old plantation and our main building was typical of the Southern mansions in the United States with their large pillars on the verandas. My medical experience with the mira users was that it affected the muscles and made them very weak. I told all the sisters, sixteen in all to hold hands tight around the large rounded columns facing inwardly under the portico. We held fast as a dozen or so Simbas arrived laughing, chanting, and promising to rape each of us several times. I kept yelling out to the sisters in French, "Tenez bien, priez et tenez bien." (Hold tight! Pray and hold tight.) "One of the men struck me on the back of the head. I was stunned but hung on. One of the other sisters yelled in my place. Over a period of time, several of my companions yelled out the encouragement. The men tugged and pulled at us, ripping our habits but they were too weak and couldn't loosen our grips. Discouraged, they promised to return as they disappeared into the darkness. We stayed thus for about a half an hour fearing that they may have tricked us."

"What did you do then? Weren't you frightened that they would come back?"

"Of course, we knew that they would return. We sent all the patients home. As you know, the African hospitals always welcome the relatives to stay in a hospice specially for them. So it was easy to send them home with their relatives. Early the next morning we left by river boat for Kinshasa. Our convents there were overflowing with sisters who had fled their stations unscathed. Some were not so fortunate. I performed many abortions on both European and African sisters who had been impregnated by the rebels over a three month period. When the religious authorities heard about it in Belgium all hell broke loose because of my un-catholic actions. Many of the lurid and graphic accounts including both black and white women who had been violated were documented in the Paris-Match magazine. But of course, the powers that be, never saw the magazine! Caught up in this quandary, I decided to escape to Basutoland."

"Why did you choose Basutoland? Wasn't that far from Kinshasa?"

"That's a whole other story. I had a brother who was an Oblate missionary there and I needed money to fly back to Belgium. I was relieved to hear that the Catholic hierarchy there had made a public statement to the religious women about the issue of violation. They stated that it was morally correct to seek medical redress."

"That was not a very avant-garde stand in my books because the likelihood of it happening in Basutoland was nil! I would have been more impressed had they taken issue with the injustice of apartheid," said Johnna bitterly.

"How long have you been working in Mbala with the Good Shepherd sisters?"

"I have been there three years but I spent three months at the Bemba Language School in Ilondola."

"Did you find iciBemba difficult to learn? I found the Sesotho of Basutoland hard because we had to speak English to the students all the time at school. Nurses have an easier time because they must address their patients in their own tongue."

"Yes, it gets easier when you spend your days with the Africans, speaking with them in their language."

Johnna went to bed with all the stories of the Congo going through her head. Sleep came soon because she was so tired.

The next day they visited Lusaka; The Legislature, the African crafts, markets, the two major hotels and the shops. She went to the Catholic secretariat to sign her contract and visited the Canadian High Commissioner.

In the morning, they were off very early. The road from Lusaka to the turn-off at Kapiri Mposhi, was full of potholes. The Great Northern Road they then took was newer and there were several lay-bys, where they could stop and rest. They stopped overnight at Kasama and arrived at Mbala before the rains began.

Johnna settled in quickly at the hospital. Not knowing the iciBemba language was indeed a great handicap; none of the patients spoke English and the African staff had difficulty communicating. When it got too frustrating Johnna went to the matron and asked about the language course.

Sister Ellen was very sympathetic but said that the Grant-aided nurses were not paid to go to the Language Course. The sisters paid for their own members and did not sign contracts individually. So if a sister was away another sister replaced her.

Johnna could not see how she could work without the language. She went to Sister Bridget with a proposition she couldn't refuse.

"Sister Bridget," Johnna said, "I have a proposition to make about my going to study iciBemba for three months in Ilondola. I cannot function as a nurse if I can't communicate. I have money from my inheritance, so I could pay my course and the board."

"That's fine, Johnna. But there is the question of your contract and who would replace you."

"I could pay for my salary replacement. In fact I could pay for the two-years of my contract as a gift to your mission."

"You are very generous indeed. How can we refuse such a generous gift? We'll make all the arrangements for payments and registration for the course."

Shortly after the rains in April 1968, Johnna was driven to Ilondola to start her three-month stint. She had purchased a VW Beetle which would be brought to Ilondala for her when it arrived in Mbala.

All the language students were gathered in the main conference room where the director greeted them.

"You are here to learn iciBemba. I hope that when you leave in three months, you will have mastered enough of the language to keep up a conversation in your work area. What I would like you to do now," said the Director, "is to mill about to greet and meet your fellow students."

"Were you ever a teacher before being a nurse?" asked an African woman.

"Why yes. You look so familiar. Could you possibly have been a student of mine in Lesotho when it was still called Basutoland? My name was Sister Johnna and I taught JC at St. Joseph Secondary in Khotsi."

"Mè, I am MaMofirifiri" Francina exclaims.

"Oh my goodness! I can't believe it. What are you doing here?"

"I am asking you the same thing. Why are you now in Zambia?"

"I left the Order in 1963, after I returned to Canada. I wanted so much to come back to Africa. The only way I could do this was to become a nurse. They were offering a two-year nursing course in Toronto for mature students, called Quo Vadis. After graduation, I found a job in Mbala through a Canadian priest on furlough. I had to pay all my own expenses. That was easy enough because I got an inheritance when my mother passed away. How were your years of study in Berkeley, California?" Are you married yet?"

"No I am not married. Since the Groups Areas Act of 1950, it is impossible for me to work outside of the Transkei, my homeland and nobody there is interested in learning French or Portuguese!"

"But what on earth are you doing here?" asked Johnna.

"I can't talk about it here. Let's mingle with the others and we'll talk later."

"All right. On the week-end I am going up to Mbala. Will you join me then? We can talk to our hearts' content. We both have so much catching up to do."

On the way to Mbala in the yellow VW Beetle, Johnna had bought, they continued to chat and reminisce.

"There's a question I asked in Ilondala that hasn't been answered yet. What will you be licensed for?"

"Remember the Sotho name that I had as a student of yours at St.Joseph's in Basutoland?"

"Why of course I do. You were called, MaMofirifiri – the mother of trouble!"

"That's right. So I will be licensed to make trouble!"

"You're not serious! Make trouble for whom? And where?"

"I will make trouble for the white racist apartheid regime of South Africa! With over two hundred and thirty laws against its black, Coloured and Indian citizens since 1948, apartheid has become a monster of domination, slavery, oppression and racial discrimination against Africans particularly. Now they have set up the Group Areas Act, we are forced to live in our land of birth or homelands. We are not allowed to live outside these areas even if we were born elsewhere in South Africa. I can't get a teaching post outside of the Transkei because I haven't lived fifteen years or more in the areas where the universities are. You and I couldn't talk as we are now because you being white can't go to the African locations outside of the towns and I can't stay in the towns. So you see why I am preparing to fight! We want freedom in our lifetime! Robert Sobukwe has helped us over the largest hurdle in our struggle for freedom—the fear and slavery mentality of the pacific older generations. At Sharpeville and Langa, where seventy-two people were killed and two hundred and eighty Africans were severely wounded by a police crackdown, we suffered the consequences of disobeying colonial laws. Internal colonialism must stop! The white man doesn't have our fear as a weapon anymore, so now he must resort to the gun. We will confront guns with guns! Sobukwe may be in prison, but his spirit lives on and moves us to struggle and win freedom in our lifetime!"

"Francina! I want to help! I want to join the Freedom Fighters with you!"

"Pompanyane! Have you forgotten your Sotho name? Blue eyes are sick eyes according to Africans. You could never pass as an African, even if you wear a traditional Basoto blanket like you used to and carry things on your head as you used to carry your books to class!"

"Whites can feel solidarity with our cause surely. What about your Russian comrades? They are not black!"

"They are not Caucasian. Their origins are Mongoloid even as ours. Sobukwe no longer believed in the politics of compromise as practiced by the old guard ANC (African National Congress) influenced by their white friends. Once he said, "Every time our people have shown signs of uniting against oppression, their white friends have come along and broken that unity.""

"Your Robert Sobukwe defined "Africans" not by the colour of their skin but by their commitment to Africa, if my memory serves me well. If you associate all white people with domination and ostracize them from your struggle, aren't you creating a black apartheid?"

"All I know is that I am committed to death, to free my people and overthrow the racist system!"

"By creating a caste system of a different colour? You know how committed to Africa I am."

"I was only eleven years old when the African National Congress launched their Defiance Campaign. I was in the riot when twenty-six Africans and six whites were killed. I was in Port Elizabeth the day the bombs started exploding in defiance. I helped kill the Dominican Sister nurse when she came to our village in the Transkei. She thought we needed her help! She was on the side of the whites. She tried to persuade us to give in. That's when I began my arms struggle."

"You must help me to join. Find out if I can train with you. I have money and I can help financially also."

"I will ask the General and then I will call you on the phone from Lusaka. Now let's go over to the museum. What is it called again? And what is the man in charge's name?"

"The museum is known as the Moto-Moto Museum and the director is Father Mukwai. You'll probably have to write to me because the phones don't always function during the rainy season in Zambia."

At the Museum, Father Mukwai greeted them.

"Father, I would like you to meet a dear friend and former student of mine from South Africa, Francina Tsolo."

"How do you do? Have you been through the Museum yet?"

"Yes Father. I have learned that you can overcome venomous snake bites. What is your power?"

"No power, he laughed. "It's this little black stone I carry with me that is my saviour."

"But it's just an ordinary flat stone!"

"Oh no! It's no ordinary stone. It has been developed by a Belgian Pharmaceutical Company. They heard of my work and asked me to try it. I am their guinea pig."

"I don't understand what you mean by "their guinea pig"?

"Well," he said, "in a laboratory they use the guinea pig, which is small animal to conduct experiments on. They are experimenting on me. If I die they fail. So far I have survived twelve serpent bites... they haven't failed."

"How do you use it? Do you rub it over the bite?"

"Yes and you leave it there for twenty-four hours. You can use a cloth or handkerchief to hold it in place, depending on where the bite is! All you have to do is wash it with soap and water to restore its effectiveness."

"Are they expensive? How much do they cost? Would I be able to buy some? How long would it take to receive them? Would they come before the next rains?"

"Whoa! So many questions! They cost about two dollars American. Yes, I could order some for you. How many do you want? How will you pay? It has to be in US dollars."

Johnna interjected politely. "Father, I will pay for them in American dollars. I have Travellers' cheques with me."

Father whistles, "Well how many do you require?"

"I would need one gross."

"I hope you are not expecting to resell them!"

"I, I … " Francina stammered hesitatingly.

"Father, there are over one hundred and fifty at her school and they are in a very swampy area near Chilange south of Lusaka. They have to travel in the bush a lot," offered Johnna.

"You're in luck, my lady. We have a Belgian Father going on home leave and he is to return long before the rains next season. Johnna could then see that you receive them as she will let you know when they arrive."

"The school authorities will be very happy and grateful to both of you."

The weeks flew by. Johnna promised to write to a mail box number in Lusaka as soon as the stones arrived. Francina promised to ask the General, if Johnna can join them. A few months later Francina received a letter from Johnna saying that the stones had arrived and she would come to Lusaka with them. By return mail Francina writes:

*September 13, 1968.*

*Dear Pompanyane, (The pretty one still!)*
*The General was furious with me for telling you about our camp until I told him what you had done for us. He asks that you bring the stones yourself. When you are here he will interview you for the possibility of joining our group.*

> *Follow, the directions on the back of this letter to find us. When you arrive at the sign that says, "Chilange School" toot your horn: one, two, three and wait. Good Luck!*
> *Francina*

In early October when the stones arrived, Johnna asked for a leave of absence from work and headed for the camp. Arriving at the designated sign, she tooted as directed. Out of the bush Francina comes out to greet her.

"Oh Modimo! Oh my God. What have you done to Seponono (The beautiful one)?"

"How do you like my disguise? I had some black stockings from my convent days. I cut out the necessary holes and slipped it over my head. I used my cashmere stockings on the head and now I have peppercorn hair! Do you think the general will like it?"

Crying with laughter Francina said, "I wish the other members of our Quest Club could see you now! And what about your former superior, Inez? The General will be impressed with your ingenuity and how serious you are about joining the Freedom Fighters."

Francina presented her former teacher to the General, who didn't know what to think.

"You are welcome Miss Rymhs. As you know you will be obliged to prove your sincerity as well as your allegiance to our cause if you are allowed to join. I understand from Comrade Tsolo that you were able to quote Comrade Sobukwe. Very commendable!

At thirty-five, you'll need a lot of stamina to keep up with the other younger trainees. The first thing you must do is to cover up your yellow Beetle before it is noticed. The South African Air Command is always making sorties across the border to bomb our installations. When you have camouflaged your car, Comrade Tsolo will take you to the Survival Sergeant for briefing."

Francina was still laughing over Johnna's disguise as they cut branches and hid the car totally. She briefly explained the honeycomb design of their subterranean quarters and left her at B-4 (Survival Sergeant) for further instructions.

The NCO at B-4 was expecting her. He explained briefly what her instructions were.

"You will spend two weeks alone in the bush—it is your survival test. You have no food or water—you will find in your booklet how and where to find both. You cannot light a fire unless you are absolutely sure that it is safe and never at night. Remember it is at the end of the dry season. Follow your map at all times; use your compass; instructions are in the booklet for that too. Needless to say you should have your black stone with you at all times. You will leave now. Do not go to your cell before you leave and speak to no one on the way out. You have two hours before sunset. Good luck!"

As she climbed the stairs of the "beehive" she heard a: "psst…. psst … Pompanyane. How was it?"

"Oh God Francina. What the hell did I get myself into? I'm off to see the wizard, the wonderful wizard of Oz! I just hope I know which mushrooms are poisonous and which aren't!"

"You'll be ok. Anyone who could survive Inez, can surmount anything! You have mastered all the skills you need when you were a Girl Scout leader in Basutoland. Now you must conquer fear … It is your only enemy. Good luck."

"You're right! Living through Inez's regime prepared me for anything"

When the two weeks were up a weary Johnna found herself before the General again at Camp Lenin.

"Well done, Makoa (The white one). Well done! Now you are ready for a special mission that only a white person can accomplish.

Two days hence," continued General Whirlwind, "you will remove all your camouflage and dress in your very best European clothes. And I might add, look your prettiest."

Johnna was deeply curious. In her life's experiences she had never felt this overwhelmed.

The general continued "Our brother Simon Kapwepwe has defected from Kenneth Kaunda's UNIP (United National Independence Party) because he refused to accept unjust practices. He formed his UPP (United Progressive Party) because of what he considered rampant hypocrisy. He claimed Kenneth Kaunda only gives lip service to sanctions against South Africa. He has declared a curfew and at eight in the evening, he sends a plane to South Africa to pick up supplies for his wife Betty's shop in Lusaka. If you walk down Independence Way, all the shop windows are empty but hers. This hypocrisy is intolerable. He also ignores the nightly raids, the S.A. Air Defence is making against our camps in Rhodesia, Zambia and Botswana. Now this is what we need you to do. I have used your small suitcase. What do you call it? a cosmetic bag? We have set up a time bomb to go off tomorrow at eleven in the morning during the parliamentary session. You will pretend that you are a tourist visiting the National Assembly and leave the case under Kaunda's chair before the session begins. Simple enough. You risk being found out. Are you prepared to take this risk for our cause? You can still change your mind."

Johnna was taken aback by such a request. She thought that the Freedom Fighters endorsed Nelson Mandela's philosophy of sabotage of buildings but not people and she asked the General if that was a departure from their mandate.

"Our mandate is "the liberation of the masses" by whatever means the High Command decides. If you are discovered, the Canadian High Commissioner would surely plead your cause and you may only be deported and not executed. Are you prepared to take on this task?"

"Yes General. I am prepared to sacrifice my life if needs be for the cause of freedom for the Africans."

"Good. You will leave immediately. The men have serviced and cleaned your car. They have also packed all your belongings in the bonnet (hood). Any questions?"

"May I see Francina Tsolo before leaving?"

"No. That is not a good idea. It may weaken your resolution to talk of your fears. I will inform her of your results. Good luck Makoa and thank you!" said General Whirlwind, as he shook hands with her.

Johanna travelled to Lusaka and nonchalently visited the National Assembly where she placed the small case under the chair as planned. Everything went off smoothly until a few hours later when she reached a road block travelling south from Lusaka. The police were able to identify the case in the bonnet as the same make and Canadian distributor as the one found under KK's desk. She was immediately brought to the airport where the Canadian High Commissioner awaited her. She could say that the case had been stolen from her hotel room at the International Hotel. The H.C. seemed to be an understanding man.

But she had never lied in her life and she couldn't put the organization in jeopardy.

A police officer approached her and said: "You are lucky that the Commissioner has pleaded for you or you might have been executed for treason. The government has declared you an unwelcome alien and we are deporting you to your village in Canada. Your government will pay reimbursement for your ticket to Toronto. Your personal belongings in Mbala will be confiscated. Endika (Thank you)"

She felt shame and pride as she approached His Excellency. The emotions were so confused and so strong that she started to cry.

"You can avoid all this if you give evidence before a court," said the High Commissioner.

Johnna looked him straight in the eye and said, "My father taught me to be true to myself above all else. Only history will prove the reason and the necessity for my actions. The governing process is not the Westernization of Africa but Africanization of the Western elements. Thank you for interceding on my behalf. I shall be eternally grateful."

"I admire your spirit. Go well Miss Rymhs."

Two years later Johanna received a note from Francina. She reads it out loud as she was accustomed to doing.

*Church Hostel. Lusaka, Zambia.*
*September, 1970.*

*Pompanyane,*

*After you were deported, Camp Lenin was bombed by the S. A. Air Command. Luckily we were all out on manoeuvres at Kariba Dam. We were dispersed and I shared a hideout with Mpho Thokwane for several weeks as the planes continued coming, night after night. During that time I became pregnant. We went back to camp only to hear that General Whirlwind and about forty others had been killed. The bombs struck the dining–kitchen areas where they were taking their evening meal.*

*One of my sister-comrades gave me some traditional African abortion medicines from the Transkei. I aborted all right but was left with an infection in the intestines that won't go away. I am very very weak from continuous diarrhea and unable to continue my guerrilla work. Mpho has been ordered to active duty in South Africa.*

*The Canadian High Commissioner who remembers you well is helping me. He thinks that I got the infection from the bush where I lived and taught. He obtained a six weeks visa on compassionate grounds for me to go to Canada to seek medical help. Please send me an air ticket to Toronto. Send it to the Canadian Embassy in Lusaka.*

*See you soon,*
*Francina.*

A few weeks later the two friends embraced at the Lester Pearson International Airport.

" Mapholeni Mukwai, (Hello Madame in iciBemba from Zambia)

"Welcome to my village," laughs Johnna.

"Do you remember the Dennis Brutus poem you taught us at St. Joseph's?" Francina asks.

Hugging each other they begin to quote,

"Somehow we survive,
and tenderness,
frustrated does not wither."

# Chapter Fifteen

Johnna has settled in Toronto where she took a job at the Sick Children's Hospital. It fulfills her need to help the underpriviledged. Many of the incurables are just left there; parents have abandoned them. She has a small apartment, frugally furnished. She is in constant contact with her three Quest Club friends, sending them parcels, money and encouragement. Most of her free time is devoted to these endeavours.

Her brother Luke lives in Willowdale, north of Toronto where he set up his veterinary practice among the wealthy. He prospered well, his family was growing but he really worried about his sister. He shared these concerns with Alan Forrest who was now a prosperous architect and had always been a good friend. Alan said that they should work on getting her out of her compulsion to work and her continued devotion to Africa.

"We'll try," Luke said.

To that effect, he phoned her that evening inviting her to spend the week-end with them. To his surprise she accepted and said she would come early Saturday morning.

Luke's girls had become teenagers. She felt so disconnected with modern youth. She really felt lost unless people talked about Africa. On Friday night however she had watched a Canadian film called "Johnny Belinda." When she told the girls that she had really enjoyed it, they said:

"Auntie you watched that?"

"Yes," she said, "and I really enjoyed it."

Well, the girls were surprised that their auntie wasn't so old fashioned and boring after all. The three of them went cycling before lunch. Again the girls marvelled at Johnna's dexterity. In the afternoon, they took her bowling and that's when the bomb fell. The older girl said innocently,

"Dad is having a party tonight in your honour and he has invited uncle Alan."

"Is that a relative of your mom's"

"No, don't you remember your childhood sweetheart Alan Forrest? He and Dad are good buddies, in fact they are golfing together right now."

She hadn't thought about Alan for so long, she couldn't recall his features or much about him.

Candidly she asked, "Is he coming with his wife?"

"No silly, he isn't married. He's still waiting for you!" the youngest niece interjected.

Johnna was overcome with emotion and embarrassment. She wanted to know if he was an architect; where he lived; where he worked, but daren't ask.

The girls sensed her embarrassment so continued each their turn.

"He's an architect and he is very rich."

"He has a beautiful home on Toronto Island. He has a big yacht too."

"Yes, we went on it once. It is beautiful."

"He has a big office in downtown Toronto, we've been there too."

"When we were small, he told us just to call him uncle because he was waiting to marry auntie Johnna. Are you going to marry him auntie?"

"He hasn't asked me yet," Johnna laughed nervously.

"Will you, if he does?"

"I'll have to think about that. I have other commitments that are very dear to me."

"Africa!" The girls said in unison.

"Well yes. But there's my work at Sick Children's too."

When Johnna saw Alan that evening she was sure that he had become more handsome than ever. He didn't look his thirty nine years.

He couldn't stop staring at her either because he thought she had become more beautiful than he remembered. After supper everybody milled about on the patio or went for a swim.

Alan approached Johnna and said,

"I'm not going to ask you ever again. It's now or never Johnna. Will you marry me?"

He had always been forthright thought Johnna. The incident with the girls that afternoon has prepared her and she simply answered;

"Only on condition that I can continue my financial assistance and support to Africa."

"Is that all you ask? You are making me the happiest man on earth. I love you, my only love."

They were wed at a simple ceremony at St. Michael's Cathedral. The only guests were Luke and his family and Irene Murphy who was still a sister teaching in Toronto. Thank God, they have a modified habit, thought Johnna.

Johnna settled into married life with her usual enthusiasm and adaptability. She stopped working and took cooking courses. They were very happy. At forty years old she had her first child, a boy. She insisted that he be called "Mora" the Sesotho word for "son".

Alan who had always been supportive of her involvement with Africa calls this the last straw. He gives her an ultimatum.

"Give him another name or we'll call it quits."

Three months later he is killed in a plane crash. Johnna inherits her second fortune. She sets up a trust fund for Mora so that at eighteen he will be financially well-off and he can pursue whatever career he wishes.

After settling the estate on Toronto Island, she gave the yacht to Luke and purchased a small three bedroom house in the "Beaches", a poor district of Toronto. Raising Mora was her most important task as she went back to work at Sick Children's Hospital. She enrolled Mora at the Montessori School as soon as he was old enough to be accepted. Johnna and one of his teachers, Suzanne Smith, became very good friends. She moved in with Johanna and Mora. Johnna didn't charge her room and board so she had an automatic baby sitter. But Suzanne became more than a baby sitter. She was a true friend to Johnna and has a great influence on Mora.

Mora graduated from St. Michael's High School at sixteen. Johnna was so proud of him. A few days after graduation, Johnna approached him to know his future plans.

"Well mom, since I want to go into the Canadian Foreign Service, I have researched the requirements. First of all I must be proficient in English and French. In the F.S. they give you 52 weeks to become proficient in French after you are accepted.

I was thinking that I could attend Carleton University for my B.A., choosing subjects that would prepare me for overseas postings eventually. I could learn French and even get a summer job as a Page in Parliament during those four years. By then I shall have reached the required age of twenty for acceptance."

"It all sound logical and well thought out, for me."

"What do you think Suzanne?"

"Mora, anything you choose it's okay by me. Your mother and I are rooting for you one hundred percent."

"Now, that we know, Sue and I will help you prepare for your first adventure on your own."

# PART TWO
## EVA

Eva Kukami is a mulatto. Her mother is a Tswana from Bechuanaland and her father is an Afrikaner. She dreams of being "declared" white, to enjoy the white man's priviledges.

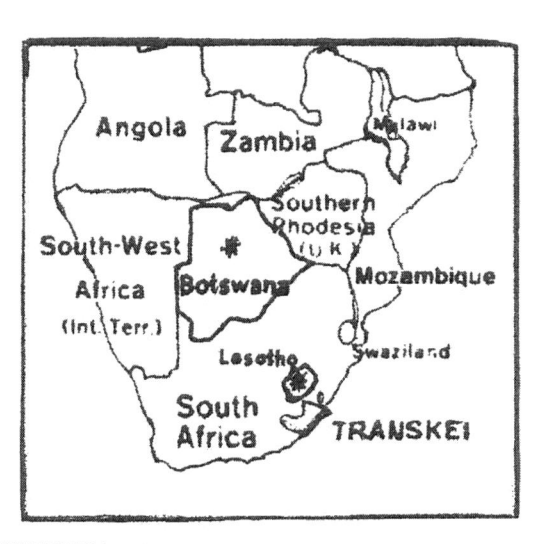

*United Kingdom*

# Chapter Sixteen
## Eva

The Negro tribes from West Africa moved eastward across the centre of the continent, in the first two centuries A.D. One of the Negro tribes, the Bantu, moved more to the south and further into East Africa. As the Bantu advanced, the Bushmen retreated to the south. The Bushmen were pushed off most of their range but kept to the hostile Kalahari Desert. The Bantu tribe that had supplanted the Bushmen in the area of Bechuanaland, was the Bechuana Tribe now known as the Botswana or Tswana. In 1885, when Bechuanaland was declared a British Protectorate, it was bounded in the north by the latitude of twenty-two degrees south. Later, the Tswana tribal rulers opposed the British government's wish to turn over the Administration of the Protectorate to Rhodesia (now Zimbabwe) in the north or to South Africa in the south. The protectorate was left under British rule until independence in 1966 under the new name of "Botswana." This is where Eva Kumani Villiers was born in 1943. As a child of miscegenation, her father an Afrikaner farmer and her mother of the Tswana tribe, she had no status. She was pale and could be accepted as white some day and work in South Africa. This was her mother's plan.

Eva Kumani sat with her mother at the back of the large farm house where they lived in Ramotswa, Bechuanaland. She often helped her mother who was the cook for the Afrikaner cattle rancher's family. Being the cook was only part of Sekone's responsibilities. She also did the housework and cared for the farmer's eight white children. Eva was now sixteen and her mother noticed that the Baas, Hans Villiers had an incestuous eye on her daughter. Eva had been sired by him and Sekona did not want what had happened to her to be thrust upon her daughter. All those years, she had saved most of her small wages to send her daughter to study in Basutoland, where the secondary school education was not watered down for the Africans as it was in South Africa. This would enable her to leave Ramotswa and work in Gabarone and even in South Africa some day.

Being of mixed race Eva was very pale and dreamed of being white. Her hair was almost straight because of the stretching she did with hot rocks from the outdoor cooking fires. Also she used whitening ointment treatments. She was very pretty and romantic by nature. Her mother noticed that the rancher was obviously obsessed with his coloured offspring. That was another reason for sending her away to boarding school.

One day Eva said to her mother: "Mother, why must I go so far away to study? I don't know anyone there."

"I have been saving my pounds sterling to give you a people's education not a Bantu education as here. I want you to have a better life than I have had."

"But I am happy to be here with you, to help you. You have so much work and if I go away you will have even more."

"For us blacks there is not much hope, child. But you are so pale that if the "Population Registration Act" passed in 1950 would change, you could have a decent life as a white person in South Africa. You would no longer have to carry identification papers recording your origins as you do now."

"But mother, I am a Tswana like you!"

"Yes, I know but we haven't gone to the government yet so they can determine on which side of the colour line you should stand. The government will decide if you are classified as white only if someone knows you in a white environment. So you must have your secretarial education so that you can get a good job in South Africa. I have put the money aside to send you to Basutoland so you can have a good priviledged life someday in South Africa."

And so it was that Eva Kumani was registered as a student at St. Joseph's Secondary School, in the Roman Catholic Mission at Khukhune, Basutoland in January 1960.

The principal of St. Joseph Secondary School introduced Sister Johnna to her students. She named them one by one and each stood and greeted Sister Johnna with, "Dumela, Mè". Johnna knew that "dumela" meant "greetings" and "Mè" was the term that meant woman or sister.

After Sister Inez left, the students began working on a simple comprehension exercise while Johnna interviewed each one privately.

"So Eva tell me a little about yourself"

"I am from Bechuanaland. My father is an Afrikaner cattle rancher and my mother is a Tswana. I use my mother's maiden name Kumani, because the Baas never married her in a church. My mother has saved her money since I was a baby to pay for my education. She wants me to be a secretary so I can get a job in Gabarone or Johannesburg and have a better life that she has had."

"Are you an only child?"

"Yes and no. I am my mother's only child but my father has eight white children. They are my half brothers and sisters."

"Have you read about the various clubs we will have as extra-curricular activities?"

"Mè, I do not understand all these new words. Can you explain them to me?"

"Yes of course, I'm sorry. A club is just another word for a group with a special activity and name. Extra-curricular means outside the regular lessons. You look at each activity being offered and seek which one you would like to belong to. All these clubs have their activities after the regular study period and each student must choose one. If you are interested in History and Geography, you can join the club I will be in charge of or any other one you want."

"Thank you, Mè, I want to join the club you are in charge of."

It became the "Quest Club" eventually and Eva became an active member.

One day, Eva became involved in an altercation with some Basuto girls. These girls had called her "a Boer," which she resented vehemently. She said she was Tswana because her Afrikaner father never married her mother in a church. Francina Tsola was sent to sort out the problem because she was tolerant and had refused to treat people as inferior if they were not of the same tribe. She happened to have been a good choice because the Basuto girls knew she was fiercely tribal and hated the Boers. After her discussion the girls never bothered Eva Kumani again.

During the school holidays in December 1961, Eva helps her mother with her work. She receives a summons from the South African government to appear before the committee to determine whether she is white or coloured.

Sekona knew that the bass would have to drive her to Pretoria and that meant an overnight stay. Sekona was worried, but she couldn't refuse her daughter as it meant her freedom from a life of slavery. She was legally the rancher's daughter by birth and the Population Registration Act was passed in 1950 to allocate racial belonging to either white, African or Coloured status. The White Areas Law stated that you were not "white" or priviledged unless you could prove that you had been born in a white environment or lived there for at least ten years and someone could attest to that and had no criminal record. The ranch was so isolated the neighbours were few and far between. The rancher did not attend church so there was no one but himself who could attest to Eva's "whiteness" and apparently that had not been enough to legitimize Eva as "white." Sekona however, had a growing feeling that the master had not wanted Eva to be white. Under the traditional conditions from the beginning of the colony, miscegenation was not only common but condoned in the form of concubinage between white men and women of colour. Three or four generations of this admixture have produced a half-caste population just a slight shade darker than some Europeans. Until "the Grand Apartheid," the Boer farmers couldn't afford to buy slaves so this practice of increasing their Bantu workers became practical as well as a source of pleasure for the males.

When Eva returned to Ramotswa with her cheap costume jewellery and some colourful toys, Secone knew instinctively how these had been got!

"And what did the magistrate say?" her mother queried.

"He put me on probation as he called it, for three more years until they make more inquiries. I have no identification documents. It will be difficult to find a job. These are just stalling tactics and I feel that my father sold me out," she cried.

Although her mother thought so too she never let on. She also knew that her baas, had had his way with her. He was too poor to be able to afford all these things for Eva. It galled her even more to think that his white children went around in rags while he spent money for his pleasure.

# Chapter Seventeen

The second year of the Junior Certificate program was well on its way. There was a white doctor in Fouriesburg, South Africa, who had a medical clinic for blacks. Johnna was not upset when two months into the term Eva asked to visit the doctor. She claimed that her mother's sister worked as his nurse and she wanted to visit her. Johnna agreed, telling Sister Inez the night before that she had two girls who needed to see the doctor when she went for the boarding school shopping. This was the usual way the students had their medical needs attended to and Inez agreed. Johnna did not query their problems.

After study that evening Johnna sat at her desk preparing lessons when there was a tiny knock at the door "Coco (May I come in?)" said the voice and Johnna answered the usual "Kena" (enter).

"Dumela, (Hello) Mè:" said Eva.

"Dumela, Eva," came the reply. "How may I help you?"

"Mè, I have big mofirifiri (troubles)."

"Do you wish to tell me about it?"

"Eh, Mè. But also I need your help and you always said that you would help us if you can."

"Yes, and I meant it!"

"During the Christmas holidays, I went to Pretoria, before the Population Registration Board to find out which side of the line I was on, white or Coloured. They gave me three years probation. That was not the problem. It was my father who took me there, where we had to stay overnight. I stayed in the van at the hotel until after midnight then he came to fetch me and sneak me up to his room. That's when he sexed me. Now for two months I have missed my moons. Yesterday, my auntie's doctor told me I was pregnant. I can't go home because my whole life will be over. I will become his slave. My mother has worked too hard for me to give up now. I need a place to stay in Johannesburg. I also need an abortion. Can you help me?"

"Whew, that's quite a problem, you poor sweetheart. I will get help for you. You must tell no one! Easter is coming with our short holiday, I think we can manage something. I have an idea."

She gave Eva a hug and told her to hurry to the dorm before lights out.

Johnna had received two hundred dollars from a retired priest in Toronto, to buy books for their library. So she asked Inez if she and Sister Irene could go to Johannesburg to buy books. They could stay with her friend Maria DeKock. Permission was granted. The plan was that Eva could help Maria with housework during the holidays and care of her children. Maria would also see to the abortion. Now Eva had tears of gratitude when Johnna and her companion left to return to Basutoland. Eva would return to school on her own the following week. Johnna advised her to write to her mother and explain the whole situation. She should write in Setswana so the master could not read her letter. Eva thanked her and said she would do that.

Maria brought Eva to her own white doctor for the procedure. He was legally allowed to do this because Eva was now Maria's domestic. Being young and strong helped Eva to recover quickly with the rest and good food found at Maria's.

She returned to school only two days late for the resumption of classes after the Easter break. No one was aware of her new situation. Her paleness was not a concern for anyone. They just thought she was using a new cream. When the other girls queried her now living in Johannesburg she just said she was living with her mother's sister. End of story.

# Chapter Eighteen

It was the last year for the JC III group. The winter holidays of June-July would be their last break before their finals in November, 1962. Eva went to Ramotswa to be with her mother.

Upon her arrival, Sekona gave her a letter from the government requiring her to appear before the committee to decide if she were white or not. Now however, she had Maria DeKock in Johannesburg who would vouch for the "whiteness" since she had lived with her during the holidays. She left after a fortnight to go to Johannesburg. This also gave her the opportunity to bring the remainder of her belongings to Maria's.

With Maria witnessing, the committee for the Population Registration in Pretoria allocated a racial belonging as white for Eva and gave her all the necessary documents. She was elated! She wrote to her mother immediately to tell her the good news, in Setswana, of course.

Once back at school in Basutoland for the final term and the final exams she sought out sister Johnna.

"Sister, Modimo (God) is good! I am not Catholic but I thank your God who has answered our prayers!"

She showed Johnna her papers. Johnna hugged her and showered her with congratulations. Now, she knew she has done right by her. Her qualms of conscience were long gone and she thanked the Lord for his sign of approval. She saw Eva's confidence and self-esteem strengthened. Maria DeKock had written during the holidays telling Johnna how happy she was with Eva. She realized that Eva would return to Bechuanaland to work and care for her ailing mother. But Maria would also be there for her and that gave Johnna great comfort. It was as though the weakest link in the circle of their friendship had strengthened them all!

When the exams were finished there was a farewell party for the graduates. Everyone at the Mission Station was invited to attend. Each of the eight graduates of St. Joseph's first graduating class was presented with a small souvenir memento which Johnna and Irene had fabricated.

At the end of the evening, they sang their favourite song for Johnna. "Kanete, kea mo rata!" "Really, I love her"!

In the morning before leaving by bus, Johnna gave her three friends an envelope with the shillings for stamps and her contact address in Toronto.

"If you ever need help write to me and I'll do what I can. I promise."

"Thank you, Mè, they chorused in unison they sang, Kanete, kea mo rata!" "Really I love her!"

Johnna would hear them long after they left when the bus rose up out of the donga up the hill to Fouriesburg and the train to Johannesburg and beyond.

# Chapter Nineteen

After the New Year celebrations in Ramotswa, early in 1963, Eva left for Gabarone to look for her first job. St. Joseph School had given each student a temporary certificate stating that they had "sat" their exams and their results would follow when they arrived from Cambridge. Johnna made sure to put Eva DeKock on Eva's certificate. Eva felt sure she would have little difficulty finding work. She stayed with her mother's sister in Gabarone's village where the Colonial Administrative Headquarters were. With her new papers from South Africa as proof of her "whiteness" and her temporary certificate from St. Joseph's she left to seek her fortune.

She took the bus into town and found the Colonial Government Administration. Nervously, she entered the building and found an information desk. The girl at the desk was Tswana. Eva had to play it cool and be aloof with her, making sure not to speak Tswana.

"Where can I find information for a job as a secretary. I have just finished my studies and am seeking employment."

Sister Johnna would have been proud of me she thought, as she waited for an answer.

The secretary went into an inner office and returned to her desk. She sat down and wrote a note which she handed to Eva. It said, "Go to Room 201 and ask to see Mr. Wickham."

"Thank you." Eva said as she hurried to find Room 201.

She tapped on the door, lightly. She entered when she heard the strong accented voice say,

"Come in."

"I am Mr. Wickham and you are?"

"My name is Eva DeKock. I am seeking my first employment. I just sat my final exams and await my results. Here are my papers."

He peruses her papers and says that they will employ her temporarily and when her results are in, they will consider permanent employment. He rises and gives her a handshake, wishing her well.

"Go to Room 208 and ask for Mrs. Langdon. She will train you in her department."

Marjory Langdon was from Pretoria originally. She came to Gabarone to be with her husband who works for the Asbestos Mining exploration company at Kanye. She is friendly and kind to Eva, who learns quickly and doesn't have to be told twice what to do.

Once back at her Auntie's in the Old Village, she is exhausted. She gives her aunt the news and after supper retires to her room where she writes to Johnna who has now returned to Canada. She explains her problem with her new identity. She had to use Maria's family name on her temporary certificate from St. Joseph but when her certificate comes from London it will have her mother's name on it. She is afraid to present it as her Colonial Government employers think she is an Afrikaner, a white South African. Although Mr. Wickham did not query the fact that St. Joseph was in Basutoland. What should she do? She signs off, saying she awaits a response.

The weeks flew by and Eva was so busy she temporarily forgot her forebodings. Then one day, as she arrived home after work her Auntie handed her letter from Toronto, Canada. She tore it open and began to read,

*"Dear Miss Eva DeKock, a.k.a. (also known as) Eva Kukami, you will find herein a temporary certificate with your new "white" name from St. Joseph Academy in Johannesburg.*

*Isn't Maria a splendid friend to you? With a slight deception she has again come to your rescue.*

*I am now out of the convent, living with my brother and going to Nursing School. When I graduate I hope to return to Africa.*

*With love and prayers,*
*Johanna"*

Tears ran down her cheeks. Her Auntie thought it was bad news.

"No, no Auntie, It is really good news"

After eight months working for the Colonial Government, things became unbearable. Co-workers kept inviting her to local parties. They kept questioning her about her family, etc.

She told them her mother, Maria DeKock lived in Johannesburg. Why was she here in this God forsaken area? They queried. She manufactured some story about her boyfriend being employed in the Agricultures and Ranching Seheme at Mahalapye. That seemed to pacify them temporarily.

The pressure from co-workers forced her to seek other employment. Now that she had almost a year's experience it was easier.

In 1966, Eva sent a copy of her Resumé to Johnna who is now a nurse working in Toronto. Johnna read it with a smile.

Name:              Eva DeKock
Birth:             1943-11-07
Place:             Johannesburg, South Africa
Education:         Primary School, St. Joseph private, Johannesburg
                   Secondary School, St, Joseph, Johannesburg
School Leaving Certificate:    Cambridge England
                               O. Level – Secretarial

Work Experience:
1. January 1963 – November 1963
   Colonial Government Office, Gabarone
              Secretary – Typist,

2. December 1963 – August 1964
   Mahalapye Agriculture School
              Secretary – Typist.

3. August 1964 – December 1965
   UK Colonial Agriculture Development Corporation, PTY Kasane
              Secretary – Typist

4. December 1965 – June 1966
   Lobatse Textiles, small family run woolen mill
              Secretary – Typist

Eva added a short letter. "My new work is now as a wife to Piet Van Zyl, the son of my boss. We will be moving to Johannesburg where Piet has a job with the De Beers Mining Enterprise."

# Chapter Twenty

Eva never had been so happy. She phoned Maria DeKock to tell her that she was pregnant. Maria was elated as though her own daughter was expecting and she is having her first grand child. She also writes to Johanna with the same news.

In September 1967, Eva gave birth to a seven pound baby boy. He was coloured. When Piet found out, he reassured Eva that to him it made no difference. But Eva knew the apartheid laws. Maria was with Eva when the baby was brought to her. She was able to influence the doctor to let her take Eva home with her. But they all knew that the hospital would have to declare this to the government.

After a few weeks, Piet's father disowned him to avoid government reprisals against himself. Though he lived and worked in Lobatse in Gabarone, he was still an Afrikaner. But Piet loved Eva and their child, whom she called John after Johnna. He had approached the South African Communist party who were the paymasters and organizers of the ANC in exile. They became committed activists against apartheid.

The organization was not for opportunists or deadwood, they were told. The African National Congress called itself a temporary home abroad and claimed to be the premier organization of the oppressed, democratic majority. The organization welcomed whites who strived to destroy apartheid and set up a true democracy in South Africa. Although they were helped by the world Communists it had to maintain itself as a liberation movement to keep receiving international support. They relied on symbols and myths such as "Africanization" and the "defeated enemy." In 1960, the Black Consciousness Movement's main purpose was to convince blacks themselves that black is beautiful." It was not important to pass to "white" to be a full citizen of South Africa, they claimed.

Early in 1968, Eva, Piet and baby John flew from Gabarone, Botswana to London, England where they were welcomed by the London based, Anti-Apartheid Movement.

The AAM found a flat for the family at the Tower Hamlets–the Heart of Old East End, and supplied Piet with a Mini-Morris.

His salary was just sustaining them so Eva got a job as Language-assistant for the British Council. The organization had babysitters which allowed Eva to go to work. Piet lead the campaign to boycott South African goods.

By the time they returned to South Africa in late 1994, Piet was fifty-four, Eva was fifty-one and John was twenty-five. They had not been sterile years. They all continued their education. Piet obtained an M.A. in Business Administration; Eva got a teaching certificate in Business Education and John followed his father, getting a B.A. in business.

They had missed the ceremonies for the installation of Nelson Mandela as the first black president on May 10, 1994. But the ANC rewarded them by giving Piet a position in the new civil service. Eva got a teaching position in a Government Business School, preparing staff for the Civil Service. John was hired by the De Beers Mining Enterprises, where his father had worked. They had settled in the new government housing in Pretoria. John had moved to Johannesburg where he worked for the De Beers Mining Enterprises.

# PART THREE
## FRANCINA

Francina Tsolo, is a Xhosa (Kosa) from the Transkei in South Africa. She joins the Youth Branch of the ANC as an active militant while still in Secondary School. She trains in Zambia at an African National Congress centre before being sent to South Africa as a Terrorist against apartheid.

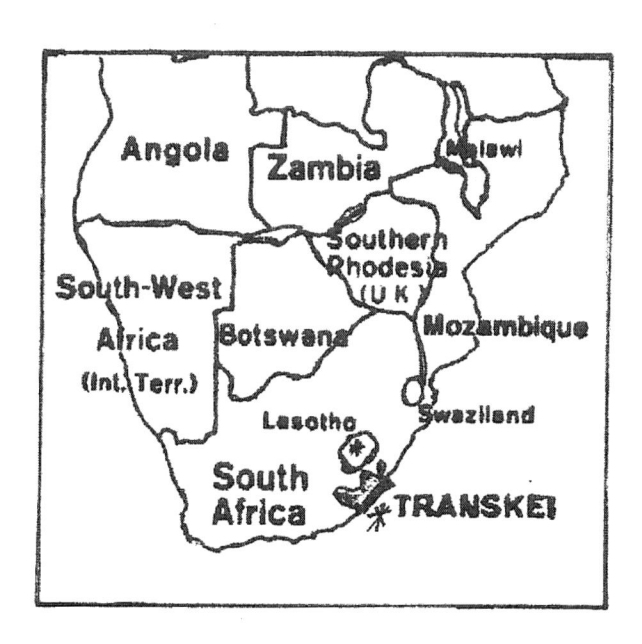

# Chapter Twenty-one
## Francina

The Transkei is a region in the Eastern Cape Province of South Africa and it literally means "the area beyond the River Kei". It is bordered by the Great Kei River in the south; the Indian Ocean on the east; Natal province on the north and the Basutoland–Drakensberg Mountains on the Northwest. Here the AmaXhosa tribes were perennially at war with the Afrikaners. In the mid 19th Century, Britain's Colonial Government at the Cape left the Boers in isolation in the "worthless" north. Britain had too many problems with her Empire Building in Ireland, the Crimea and India.

The AmaXhosa themselves put an end to the problem. One of their prophetesses, a young girl who had visions from ancestors, persuaded the tribesmen that they could at last defeat the whites, by raising their warrior ancestors from the dead. She convinced them to sacrifice all their cattle and burn their crops and that would bring their ancestors back to life!

The sun would turn in the sky, a hurricane would sweep across the land and the dead would rise with spears and push the invaders into the sea, when that happens their cattle and crops would be re-incarnated. History tells us that thousands died of starvation and others travelled south to white farm owners to seek food and work. That's how they became more dependent on agriculture than cattle as before.

Britain had left the Boers alone in the hostile north until the "Star of Africa", an 83.25 carat diamond was found on a farm near the Vaal River in the present Orange Free State. With the whites all flocking to the mines, the Xhosa tribes were left alone in their tribal areas. The men soon found more money going to work in the far-away mines. This enhanced their economy but broke up the families!

In 1941, in the small town of Libode, near Umtata, Francina Tsolo was born. As was the Xhosa custom she was given the tribal name of Noxolo which meant Peace. Her tribal name was really a misnomer. She was self-opinionated and quick-tempered but proud of her tribal roots and passionate about removing the yoke of the Boers who held power. She was outspoken about apartheid.

She hated her paternal grandfather, an Afrikaner shopkeeper in Umtata, who sired her father with his white children's Xhosa nanny. She joined the youth Organization of the ANC and PAC, both formed to oppose apartheid, long before they launched their Defiance Campaign. She was involved in the riots when twenty-six Africans and six whites were killed in Port Elizabeth. She was among the youths who tried to stop them.

By the time she was a student at St. Joseph's in Khukhune, Basutoland, she had developed a deep desire to be a freedom fighter. Her fellow students had named her MaMofirifiri – the Mother of troubles. Johnna, who recognized her potential encouraged her to apply for a scholarship in America. In 1963, she applied and obtained a scholarship to study Linguistics at U.C.L.A. In September of that year, she arrived in Los Angeles for the next phase of her life. All the while, she kept in contact with Johnna in Canada by letter or by phone.

# Chapter Twenty-Two

Liberal Francina felt right at home on the U.C.L.A. campus of the sixties. The Kennedy era brought great changes. The Civil Rights Movement also brought hope for the blacks, especially in the southern U.S. The Black Power Movement reminded Francina of their struggle against apartheid. It surprised her that the blacks in America were still struggling for full integration. She joined various groups on campus that would enlighten her and help her shore up ideas for her political future once she returned to South Africa. But she preferred the communist group by far. She writes to Johnna who was now studying to be a nurse in Toronto.

*5th October, 1963.*

*"Dear Pomponyane,*

*I am really enjoying my time here at U.C.L.A. I had not realized how similar the struggle for the blacks here was to ours. From what I can gather we are far happier in our home life in the Transkei!*

*There are a host of avenues via clubs and movements that I can join to get ideas to use once I am back working with the ANC Youth League back home.*

*I've joined the Black Consciousness Movement and the Black Power Movement. Most important to me however is the Communist Youth Group. I do avoid the drug scene and communes. The countercultural groups with their way-out dress, songs and music really don't appeal to me either. But I have joined an all-black choir group. I avoid clashes because the administration is afraid and powerless, vis-à-vis these groups. The students disrupt classes or lecturers; demand that the curriculum be changed etc. So it is easier for administrators to ignore smaller issues and keep the peace.*

*L.A. has become a city of communes, where drugs flow and civil disobedience seems to be the order of the day. Sexual preferences are exploited publicly and dress, songs and music are countercultural, to say the least.*

*About coming up to Canada, to visit you at Christmas, that is out of the question, it is too cold! During the summer I am taking courses to speed up the time to graduation, I hope to have my PhD. by June 1967.*

*Keep well, Seponono,*

Your former student and present friend,<br>Francina Tsolo.

# Chapter Twenty-Three

The jet landed at Jan Smuts airport at precisely four in the afternoon of June 10, 1967. After all the whites had deplaned, the blacks were allowed to descend. The blacks boarded a bus that drove them to the airport. At the section reserved for blacks a small group from the Tsolo family were there to welcome Francina. Her father was the first to hug his daughter. They were all so proud of "Doctor Tsolo."

Once back home at the family kraal, Francina unpacked her suitcases. She had gifts for everyone; her father, mother, brothers and their wives, her sisters and their husbands and of course all the nephews and nieces! When the pandemonium was over and everyone had enjoyed the feast, Francina dropped the bombshell. She was leaving for training with the ANC terrorists. Everyone was stunned by her news. When was she leaving? How was she going? Who was she going with? Where was she going? When was she leaving?

"I can only say that I am leaving on Monday."

"Monday!" they exclaimed in unison. "Why so soon?"

"You all know that I am a member of the military wing of the ANC. I have been since 1959. For years, the ANC was banned. Our leaders went into exile and set up the military wings and training camps for terrorism. The Chinese Communists funded and supported groups in Lybia, Tanzania, Rhodesia and the Russian Block is supporting groups in Algeria and Zambia mainly. I am going to train as a terrorist; that's all I can tell you."

Her father put his arm around her shoulders and said in Xhosa, "Do what you have to do, my child and God be with you!"

On Monday morning, she left her home kraal early in the morning and took the first bus for Umtata. There she boarded another bus to Johannesburg, where she arrived late in the afternoon. There was a minibus to pick her up and take her to the Soweto Township where the new headquarters of the underground military wing of the ANC had been relocated. They had set themselves up in several houses on different streets. There were several new recruits assembled at what was called "Freedom House" After a meal had been served, they attended a briefing..The six in Francina's group were driven by Kombi (10 seater VW bus) to their house for the night. Once there, they were asked to choose a leader. When they found out that Francina had studied in America and had a doctor's degree, she was chosen. After she had accepted, the comrade leader gave her an envelope with similar instructions she had received in Los Angeles. "Memorize then burn." She thanked the comrade and he left. They were on their own now. Everyone was so tired that they all agreed to go to bed now and meet at nine in the morning.

At sunrise, she slipped her clothes on and went outside where she read her instructions. It contained one typewritten page.

*June 18, 1967.*

*Comrade Leader of Cell 431*
*Read these instructions to your Cellmates then burn.*
*Orders: Leave Soweto on morning of 20th by minivan at your door at 6.00 A.M.*
*You will travel to Mafeking where you will change into the Tswana clothing, especially the two women.*
*You will cross into Botswana with a herd of cattle going to the market at Lobatse. This is north-east of the border station manned by the South African Police.*
*You will carry only your South African Pass document, no photos, no letters.*
*From Lobatse you are to travel on your own as far as Kasane, near where the Zambezi River joins the Chobe River in the Caprivi Swamps, briefly forming a border with Botswana and Zambia. Your comrades there will get you across the river to Kazungula, Zambia where comrades again will meet you. They will drive you to Kafue where General Whirlwind himself will meet you and bring you to Camp Lenin in south-eastern Zambia.*
*Burn this document.*

After studying the document, the new recruits left as planned. They reached Kafue, Zambia nineteen days later. They were met by General Whirlwind, Commander–in–charge of Camp Lenin in South Eastern Zambia.

# Chapter Twenty-Four

General Whirlwind was a huge man, of Idi Amin stature. He shook hands with each cell member as they gave their name.

"Who is your cell-leader?" he asked.

"I am" replied Francina.

"What is your tribal name?"

"It is Noxolo and it means peace in Xhosa," she replied but at school in Basutoland I was called MaMofirifiri, which means the Mother of Trouble in Setho. It is more accurate!"

He gave a hearty laugh and said to all of them, "Here at Camp you will be called by your family name."

Their large jeep-like vehicle bounced on the rutty, pot-holed bush roads at a fast speed. All of a sudden they turned off and the General parked the vehicle in a large lean-to covered with branches and leaves held together with dried mud.

There were six camouflage-clad comrades who came to greet them but didn't say a word.

Finally, General Whirlwind told them in English to take the new recruits to their rooms adding that they should wait for them and in a half hour bring them to the conference room for briefing.

The conference room was large, with several classrooms and reading rooms appended. All the walls were covered with shelves of books.

Everyone stood when the General arrived with a retinue of camouflage-clad comrades.

"Comrades, Welcome to Camp Lenin. You have come from various front-line states. Some of you are from Rhodesia, where the Salisbury government has declared an illegal independence by declaring UDI in 1965. Our Rhodesian comrades are trying to rid their country of the racist regime of Ian Smith. Many of you are from various regions of South Africa, even as myself. We all have a common purpose with our communist collaborators, which is the liberation of the masses. We have a common, direct bond with our compatriots. We do not believe in the politics of compromise anymore! Last year, Verwoerd was assassinated but nothing has changed. In fact the racists are more brutal than ever!"

"Ubuntu" is what we want for every African on the continent! In Sotho, we say that "Ubuntu" is motho ke motho ka batho"—a human being with, by, and for human beings! That's what we are fighting for, Comrades. Mayibye i Africa! Let Africa return!"

"Mayibye i Africa! Let Africa return!" the trainees chanted.

"Would Comrade Francina Tsolo report to my office after the assembly. Company dismissed!"

Francina turned to her neighbour and said, "Where is the General's office? The compound is so large, I have no idea."

"I will be glad to show you. My name is Mpho Thokwane. I am also Xhosa. I learned the layout very quickly because when my brother returned from Zambia, he drew it for me. Presently he is with a sabotage crew in Soweto."

"Thank you, very much. As you know my name is Francina Tsolo."

Mpho continued, "Our whole network of operations is well thought out. It works like the cells of a honey comb. I will give you the diagram tomorrow. For now I will guide you to the General's office."

"That will be kind of you."

"Didn't you see that big notice as you approached the conference room, [The Queen H-5]?"

"No," replied Francina

"It stands for the Queen Bee—the one in charge. Mine by the way is C-5. What's yours?

"Mine is A-1. "Neat eh?"

"Real neat. My bro told me that all the number "Ones" clean the latrines!"

"Thanks a lot!" she says as she knocks on the office door. "Koko." (Permission to enter.)

From within, "Kena!" (Come in). "Ah comrade Tsolo. You must be wondering why I have sent for you?"

"I am a bit mystified, sir."

"I have been studying my files in order to best use the capabilities of our new recruits. I discovered that you have a doctorate in Languages from Berkeley, California. You must have studied semantics which gives you a facility for languages."

"I majored in French and Portuguese," sir.

"That's very impressive. But why aren't you teaching in South Africa?"

"You realize, sir, that in 1959, the extension of the University Education Act reduced Fort Hare University to a Tribal College. Our great leaders had been educated there before it was watered down."

They have no need for linguistics studies other than the African dialects. Mr. Mandela published his "Umkhonto We Sizwe" manifesto in 1961 following the Sharperville-Langa massacre. I was still in high school when I promised myself to join the military wing of the ANC."

"Ah yes! The great Mandela! The Black Pimpernel!"

"You know our champion, then?"

"Yes, we did our guerilla training together in Algeria in 1962. Now that he is in prison, we must not let him down, "Umkhonto We Sizwe" may be dead but the Youth League is not. Now, the reason for which I called you. During the rainy season which starts late in November and lasts until April, many of our trainees die from snake bites received in manoeuvres in the bush, I have heard that there is a Canadian priest who has a museum at Mbala, in the Northern Province. You will go to the Ilondala Language School and study iciBemba. While there, you will make your way to Mbala and befriend this Father and obtain from him the power he has to overcome venomous snake bites that he captures for his museum. They say he has been bitten nine times and survived with his magic. The language course lasts three months. You should be back before the rainy season begins. You will leave tomorrow by train from Lusaka to Kapiri Mposhi where comrades will pick you up and drive you to Ilondola."

"You are bound to secrecy about your work and your training here at the camp. All the Father needs to know is that you teach in a bush school near Chirundu, southeast of Kafue and you lose students every rainy season to snake bites. Ke pheto! That's all. Is that understood?"

"Yes General."

Francina made her way to the iciBemba language school at Ilondala and by a twist of fate met Johnna Rymhs, her former teacher from St. Joseph's in Khukhune, Basotoland. Johnna had left the order and become a nurse. She was presently at Mbala where General

Whirlwind had asked Francina to see about the powers of a certain priest to combat snake bites, especially in the bush.

After explaining to Johnna her work with the Freedom Fighters and the need to protect the comrades from dying of snake bites while training in the bush. Johnna helps her with money, etc. When the black stones arrive, Johnna delivers them in person with the hope of becoming an associate member of the Military Wing of the A.N.C. She succeeds but is captured after placing a bomb in the House of Assembly in Lusaka to try to assassinate Kenneth Kaunda. She is deported and returns to Toronto.

All the general told Francina was that she had been deported to her village in Canada. Johnna had given her the Toronto address and phone number if she ever needed help.

In September 1970, after the bombing of Camp Lenin, Francina and Mpho spent several weeks in a hideout and she had become pregnant. She had received tribal medicine from Xhosa girlfriends at the hideout where they awaited instructions. It was an old wives concoction of salmonella bacteria which rids the body of the fetus but causing a poisoning of the intestines that left her with continuous diarrhea.

Mpho was ordered to active duty and Francina had sent a letter to Johnna asking for medical help. Johnna asked her to come to Toronto with the help of the Canadian High Commissioner in Lusaka. She was given a six-weeks passionate visa to visit Johnna and receive medical care through the Canadian High Commissioner.

The time in Toronto fled by but she was fully recovered and her six weeks were coming to an end. Johnna had contacted Eva in London by phone to make sure she could receive Francina for a few days on her return to South Africa.

# Chapter Twenty-Five

Francina said to Johnna the day before her departure for South Africa in February 1971, "Mè, that man Alan really has eyes only for you. Will you marry him? You need someone to care for you."

"He hasn't asked me yet," she laughed nervously. "Don't forget to give my love to Eva and her family when you meet them in London. Tell her she should come for a visit also."

"Yes, there are so many beautiful things to see in "your village", she laughed, "I think you should marry Mr. Alan, you are becoming an "nkono" (an old lady), you know.

Johnna defended herself but she was well aware of age creeping up on her, but didn't like to think about it.

Johnna prepared a suitcase of clothes for four year old John; some clothes for Eva and some for Piet which Francina could take to them.

"You certainly meant what you said when we graduated from St. Joseph's in Khukhune, that you would always help us. We have all been recipients of your kindness and generosity. I think that you need a new African name now. "MaThuso" is very fitting. It means the "Mother of help."

The trip to London went smoothly. When Francina arrived at Heathrow Airport and deplaned, she proceeded to retrieve her luggage. With a cart full of cases she made her way to the arrivals lounge. She waited for over a half an hour and was about to leave when a four-year old toddler pulled on her skirt and said,

"Dumela, (Hello), MaMofirifiri!"

She was overwhelmed and a bit bewildered when she noticed Eva and Piet laughing at her bewilderment.

The ladies hugged and cried and hugged again. It had been eight years! So much had happened to both of them that for three days, they talked and talked and talked some more.

Francina, one day said, "I have given our friend Johnna a new name. She is now "MaThuso".

She has helped all three of us as she promised. She has a man friend and I think they will be married soon."

"Married? Are you joking?"

"No. He is her childhood sweetheart, who is a very rich architect from her home village. He has never married and has always loved her. Now he lives in Toronto and through her brother Luke, who also lives in Toronto, they have met again."

"Oh! That would be so wonderful," Eva exclaimed, "What are you, yourself going to do now?"

"I am going to live up to my name, I will be "the mother of troubles" for the Boers."

# Chapter Twenty-Six

When Francina arrived at Jan Smuts Airport in early 1971, she is met by Mpho Thokwane who has cleared her re-entry into South Africa. Then Mpho takes her to an ANC hostel in Soweto. The following day, he takes her to the ANC District Commandant.

"Dumela, (Hello)" comrade Tsolo. I hope you have rested well after your long trip?"

"Yes Sir. Thank you."

"I have assigned Comrade Thokwane to be your shadow until you are re-assigned to active duty. He will be the liaison between us, because we try to minimize activity here in Soweto to confuse both the South African Defence Force who are always on the prowl, day and night, as well as the good citizens who can be made to talk by intimidation. For these reasons we keep a low profile and often use code to confuse them. Mpho here is familiar with these new, necessary measures, so he will keep you informed on a "need to know" basis. Your first assignment will be to teach at the elementary school in this neighbourhood. Mpho will arrange interviews with the administration etc. They do not know anything about you except that you are his fiancée. Are there any questions? "

"I think all is understood. Thank you, sir."

She left the Commandant's office with her "Shadow." Once back at the hostel, they sat down to a cup of bush tea.

Mpho said, "Francina, you know that I love you. The Commandant said that since we are of the same tribe and we are in such close collaboration, we could get married. What do you say, will you marry me?"

"Dear, dear Mpho. You know that I love you but I cannot marry you. There's not that certainty, that true love and that commitment we must have to make a marriage work. Let's just say that I am not ready."

"But you're thirty now. If we want a family we must start soon."

"Having a family is very impractical in the work we have dedicated ourselves to. Since we do not know where our assignments will take us in the future, I fail to see how it will work. I am really sorry."

That night Francina wrote to Johnna.

*Soweto, April 1971.*

Dear MaThuso,

My stay with the Van Zyl's was wonderful. Piet is studying Business Administration. Eva got a Teacher's Certificate in Business Education. Little John is a gem and very intelligent. He is of light hue like his mother and cute as a button. They deeply appreciated your gifts, haholo (a lot). They do miss South Africa very much.

I arrived safely in Johannesburg and Mpho was at the airport to meet me. I am staying in Soweto and will be teaching Standard VI (Grade 8) in the new term in July. That's the only job available to me and still smart under the hurt that no matter how educated I am I can never be accepted into the white society on an equal basis. I cannot visit my family in the Transkei for fear of being caught! Someday, I will rediscover my own culture as H.I.E. Dhlomo did in the "Drums of Africa (1944).

Mpho has asked me to marry him but though I love him dearly it is not the "marriage love" so I said no. Also I remember our discussions back in St. Joseph's about marrying someone of similar education so that there is a common bond upon which to create a real relationship. And of course, in our present situation it would be extremely impractical even with the contraceptives you furnished me with while in Toronto.

I hope to hear soon that you and Mr. Alan are an "item" now?

Love as ever,
MaMofirifiri
P.S. Use the Post Box # on the envelope for return mail.

Francina took her teaching job seriously. Her students were always trying to get her off topic, to talk about the situation in South Africa. It was very difficult for her to pretend that she was just a serious school marm not interested in politics. She could not teach the values or the culture of the European past as she had been taught, it would put her on forbidden ground. She had to pretend she had an Afrikaner slant on the situation.

In 1976, thousands of students in Soweto held demonstrations to protest the new law, making Afrikaans the language of instruction. Police arrived with dogs, fired tear-gas and live bullets at the fleeing children. Government reports claimed twenty-five children had been killed and two hundred injured.

Within days, rioting spread throughout the country and by 1977 thousands had been injured and five hundred and seventy-five killed. The will to resist had broken the old mold of accommodation and compliance. In 1977, the South African Government adapted its Total Strategy policy to counteract the external and the internal threats to its so-called legitimate security concerns. The black militants increased their sabotage.

Francina lost her teaching job and was called to active duty. Along with Mpho and four other cell members they were involved in nightly sorties. At first they struck isolated police outposts. Then they struck beer stores, post offices, bars, restaurants, etc. causing as much destruction as possible.

One night Mpho announced to the cell members assembled for their orders;

"Tonight we hit the big one. We are to sabotage the SASOL petroleum complex."

To all the yipees and shouts of joy, he added, "You each have a role to play and you must follow your instructions carefully for complete success. As usual you read your instructions, memorize them and burn your papers."

"Are we all ok with that?"

Each one answered yes in rotation. For three hours they studied, discussed and coordinated. They interpreted the diagrams, discussed the cooperation needed, set their watches. At twelve o'clock they left in an old battered VW Minibus. They used the back roads and arrived unseen. Their sabotage was successful; three refineries had been damaged and an estimated 7.5 M dollars of damage caused. As they read the papers the next day, they proudly congratulated each other. The Koeberg nuclear station was also sabotaged in 1980. Their orders now were to separate and await further instructions.

Francina and Mpho listen to the radio and are happy to hear of all the rioting spreading throughout the country. Suddenly there was a knock on the door. "Who could that be at this early hour? Asked Mpho, "Get into bed and pretend to be sleeping. I'll answer."

He went to the door, all along feigning a half asleep state.

"Who is it?" he asks in a muffled voice.

"Wolf" he answers as a South African armoured car whizzes by.

"Commandant!" exclaims Mpho as he lets him in.

"They are searching for us. We have to escape now."

Francina got up as soon as she heard the code name Wolf.

"Gather your things; leave nothing behind. We will burn what we do not need before we cross the border into Botsawana."

The three of them left in the old battered Volkswagon bus and headed north. They crossed the border at sunrise. When they arrived at Gabarone they made their way to the ANC quarters there, in the old town.

The following day Francina left in a jeep with a comrade while Mpho was nowhere to be seen. She knew the rules: ask no questions, just follow orders.

On the way north, the driver gave Francina an envelope which she opened immediately and read,

"Comrade Tsolo,

You and your group have had a marvellous success but unfortunately you have been recognized by some of your students from Soweto who were tortured into having to identify you in the whereabouts of SASOL, the night of the sabotage. We are sending you to a town in northern Zambia called Mpika. There is a girl's secondary school there and President Kaunda himself has asked that they take you in as a secondary school teacher. You will stay there until further orders. Good luck and thank you from Mandela himself. Please burn this before you cross the border. The sooner the better."

# Chapter Twenty-Seven

After the sabotage of 1982, the government became more brutal and the rioting spread throughout the country. In 1986 a State of Emergency was declared. The ANC saboteurs were hunted down and thousands were imprisoned as the police crackdown intensified.

Francina stayed in Zambia until 1990, when the ANC in exile began returning to South Africa. Mandela was released from prison after twenty-seven years. The Soviet union ended all funds for the ANC from that source. Many of the two hundred and thirty-one measures made into laws in the name of apartheid in the 1950's and 60's were abolished.

When Francina arrived at Jan Smuts airport in Johannesburg, the ANC comrade that picked her up was a stranger.

"I have orders to drive you to your home village in the Transkei. You will stay there until further notice."

He then proceeded to tell her all the news about the political changes taking place.

She asked him if he knew Comrade Mpho Thokwane. When he said yes, she asked,

"Do you know where he is?"

"Yes Comrade. He has been jailed since 1983 when he was caught."

"Do you know where? Has he been in jail since then?"

"They keep changing his jail, so no one really knows where he is. Even his own family don't know his whereabouts."

"How horrible. I had no idea. Eight years."

At her home village of Libode there was much ullulation (African women's wailing) when she was recognized. Her father, now in his eighties was the first to welcome her. Then her mother and all her family greeted her one by one. There were a few new children she had not yet met. She was forty-nine now—too late for children of her own, she mused.

After a few days of celebration, Francina asked her senior brother to take her to Umtala to visit the Thokwane family.

She was overjoyed to hear that Mpho had been released from jail but had lost his eyesight. She hugged him tenderly when she met him but soon felt his reticence. He took the hand of a young woman and said,

"Francina, this is my wife, Florina and our son Kumali."

"Congratulations to both of you and may you be happy, is my wish. Maybe we will meet again at ANC functions. Who knows? Good bye then."

She was very quiet on the way home and her brother queried her about it.

"When we were in Zambia, Mpho and I had a child together which I aborted to remain with the freedom fighters. When I saw that baby today it reminded me of what I had lost. In the 1980's when we came back from Zambia, Mpho proposed marriage to me and I did not have wife-love for him so I said no. He has a beautiful wife and child. Myself, I would die in a small village."

"I know that and I fear the day when you will leave us again." Her brother said sincerely.

In 1994, Leala, Francina's favourite twelve year old niece brought her a letter from Pretoria. She thanked the child and opened the letter. She read her letter from ANC's Central Committee

*Pretoria S. Africa.*
*May, 1994.*

*Dear Miss Francina Tsolo,*
*We have been advised by our new ANC Central Committee to invite you to a special meeting of our Annual General Meeting. Our new President, Nelson Mandela wishes to thank you in person for all your work for the ANC over the years. This will be held at 10 a.m., May 24th, 1994 at our headquarters in Pretoria.*

*Yours in comradeship,*
*Justin A. Mbotha.*

When Francina boarded the bus in Umtata on May 23rd, many of her family were there. Though her father and mother had not made the journey.

At that fateful meeting, President Mandela shook her hand and thanked her for her dedication and good work. As he handed her a letter with her name embossed on it, he said,

"Please continue your dedication and hard work in my new government."

That evening Francina wrote to Johnna in Toronto.

*Pretoria, South Africa.*
*May 24, 1994.*

*Dear MaThuso and Mora,*

*Greetings from Pretoria. I hope all is well with you both. Pass my greetings to your brother Luke and your companion Suzanne Smith.*

*After returning from my forced exile in Mpika, Zambia where I taught school, I lived in my home village. I travelled one day to Umtata where I found Mpho who had been imprisoned for eight years. He lost his sight while there and we didn't talk about it. He has a pretty wife and is the father of a baby boy they called Kumali. They seem happy and I am peaceful about it also.*

*And for my news I have been named Minister of Education in the new government and will represent one of the Transkei seats. If you don't hear from me often, know that I am just too busy!*

*Other good news, the Van Zyls are back on native soil. Piet is Deputy Minister of Economic Development and Eva is in charge of the Secretaries' Pool. Even "John" is now employed by the De Beers Conglomerate. So you see we are all doing well in our new freedom.*

*Keep well,*
*MaMofirifi*

In 1994, Francina turned fifty-three. She had spent all her adult life towards one goal—freedom for the Africans in South Africa. Everything in her life had been sacrificed to that one goal. According to her traditions however, a woman could become a mother without that love and commitment that she had sought. When she turned in her AK-47 she felt an emptiness, she had never felt before. She felt her childlessness! Johnna had always told her that thing always worked for our good if we trusted the powers that be. But her age now gave her little hope of finding fulfillment. The dismantling of apartheid was a long, arduous task ahead of them. She had traded in her single-mindedness about her tribe for a new plurality of allegiances. The natural African philosophy and way of life was best stated in a Zulu maxim, "umuntu ngumuntu nga bantu" which means "a person is a person through other persons."

Her dear father had taught her that! In other words this expresses the basic respect and compassion for others. She had to redirect her thinking.

She could hear Johnna's voice saying "I told you so," when she met the tall handsome Daniel Makidisi at a conference one day. She felt like a silly schoolgirl when their eyes met across the table. During a coffee break he came over and introduced himself.

"Minister Tsolo, I am Daniel Makidisi. I am the Dean of African Languages at the English University of Johannesburg.

"I am very pleased to meet you Mr. Makidisi. I did my PhD in French and Portuguese at U.C.L.A. in the States"

"Yes, I saw the write-up about you in the papers, on your appointment as Minister of Education. My congratulations! They did not mention a Mister Tsolo so I assume, it is alright for me to invite you to dinner tonight?"

"I would be delighted. Here is my card. You may pick me up at seven p.m.

When she got home, she phoned Eva and told her about Daniel. She would call Johnna in the morning. She was so excited, she sang in the shower.

It was a short courtship. Daniel's son Khabane (The Warrior) was the ring bearer and six-year old Nyakallo (Joy) was her only bridesmaid.

When Francina called Johnna to tell her the news she said,

"Who would have thought that the-powers-that-be, would have found me a ready-made family?" They both laughed.

# PART FOUR
## VERONICA

Veronica Mohlana (Moshlana) is a Mosuto born in Soweto near Johannesburg. She teaches her people how to free themselves of the yoke of apartheid by the independence afforded by educating themselves how to pool their resources and build co-operatives in their own land and thus become self-sufficient. She is killed by a government sniper at a University rally.

Soweto is a Black township twenty miles from Johannesburg.

# Chapter Twenty-Eight
## Veronica

On Easter Sunday, April 23rd, 1940, cries of a new born broke the early quiet of the morning. Tumelo (Faith) Mohlana grinned broadly as he announced to the mid-wives that his sixth child should be called "Ma Paseka" (The Mother of Easter). His wife Matseliso (Consolation) had at last, after five sons, given him a daughter. Tumelo himself was born into a very religious family in Morija, Basutoland, where the Paris Evangelical Mission Society had their headquarters. It was due to their influence that his father named him Tumelo which meant Faith. True to his name, he raised his family according to the tenets of the faith of the P.E.M.S. When the newborn was baptized she was given the Christian name Veronica.

She was two years old when her mother passed away. When she was six, her father died in a mining accident in Benoni. Her older brother Joseph who had just gotten married, took care of his sister while his four brothers found homes with other relatives as was the custom.

Veronica did very well in elementary school in Soweto but Joseph realized that she was brilliant and sent her for further education in Basutoland for her Basutoland Teacher's Primary Certificate (BPTC) at Mazenod. While on holidays in her final year, she discussed with him the possibility of further education.

"Where can I teach when I finish here?" she asked him, I can't stay in Basutoland alone, nor can I teach in Soweto."

"I have been thinking about that and am prepared to pay for your further studies in Lesotho. I have enrolled you at St. Joseph, Khukhune for the next term. I will pay for three years, then we will decide what to do when the time comes."

Although Veronica was not very demonstrative, she was teary-eyed when she said,

"Kea lebua haholo, Abuti." (Thank you very much, older brother).

So she found herself in St. Joseph's Secondary School in Khukhune in January of 1960. It was here that her life ambitions came to light and were nurtured by a Canadian religious teacher name

Sister Johnna. The exchange of ideas with the five other girls and two young Basuto Sisters in her class, re-inforced her dream. One day she approached Sister Johnna as she sat at her desk and said,

"Mè, you remember when I first came here, I asked you why you were white and I was black? You said that I was C-cubed. I had circumstance, colour and culture. I have thought about that a lot and since I am not Catholic I cannot become a Sister so I must look elsewhere to fulfill my dream of helping my fellow-Basuto. I want to dedicate my life to bringing hope amid despair. I want to go to the grassroots in the villages and teach them to better their lives socially, economically and spiritually."

"That is a very noble and generous cause. First you must learn all you can to prepare yourself for the opposition you will encounter in your endeavours. The future belongs to those who believe in the beauty of their dreams. A goal is a dream without a deadline. The poet Khalil Gibran said, "When you are born, your work is placed in your heart." I remember the poem you passed me last year in which the author states, "The bird does not sing because it has to, but because it has a song." Do you remember?"

"Eh, Mè, and thank you. You have enlightened my way."

After Veronica left, Johnna fetched her "billycan" and entered in her notes: "Veronica's ambitions are realistic. She will go a long way in helping her people."

# Chapter Twenty-Nine

In January 1963, Veronica got a local scholarship to attend Morija Secondary School to complete her senior matriculation, or Cambridge A-levels. With success in these exams she could then apply for a scholarship to study abroad. She would be twenty-five when she sat her Cambridge Overseas A-level exams to obtain her senior matriculation.

She befriended a classmate, Celeste Nkosi, who was the daughter of the Reverend Thomas Nkosi, one of the clerics. This young woman was only twenty-one but like Veronica she was an avid reader and over the two years they became constant companions. They had both joined a clandestine movement called the African Feminist Thinkers. Veronica was from an urban area whereas Celeste had been born and lived all her life on the church compound at Morija. In the African tradition, women were systematically subordinated and they both agreed that education was the only avenue that released them from the dedicated African role of wife, child bearer and relative slave.

One day Celeste said to Veronica, "I try to understand why I cannot accept my traditional role. I seem to have two yokes around my neck. One is the feminine African role and the other the religious one that my family expects of me. The difficult thing is that I am not prepared to follow either."

"One of my teachers at Khukhune, a Canadian Catholic Sister, once quoted the poet Kahlil Gibran to me," "When you are born, your work is placed in your heart," she said. She further said, "When the student is ready, the teacher will appear." You must follow your dream, Celeste. It won't be easy but you will know peace."

"You are so wise. You always put me on my path whenever I get scared. I've never been very far from the mission but I want to study overseas. Please pray that my father agrees. He has already picked a groom for me—whom I can't stand!"

"My friend, Sister Johnna used to always say, "For those who trust things always workout." The Lord knows your path and he sees to it that you will follow it—just trust the Powers-that-be."

"Why don't you say "God"?

"Because, I believe that to reach all people whatever their religious allegiances, we must leave behind our differences and dwell on what unites us. We are all one in the Spirit who lives in every living thing. Sometimes if we use the name God or Christ, people whose deity has another name are turned off and we can't help them."

"What an interesting concept. I read in the archives in our museum that the first missionaries who came from France in 1833, called the mission, Morija, because it was the name that Abraham gave to the mountain where he was reprieved from killing his son. It means "God will provide."

'Surely Abraham used the Jewish word not Morija." Veronica continued,

"The missionaries who came to Basutoland, were of the Paris Evangelical Mission Society (PEMS) in 1833; the Roman Catholics (RCM) in 1862; the English Church Mission (ECM) in 1875; they were all agents of imperialism. Christianity was part of their colonial legacy. They believed that they had started formal education in Basutoland. There was however, an ongoing system of indigenous education already in place. That was the initiation rites (Lebollo). These rites were separate for men and women. They were group activities to introduce them into adulthood and lasted about six months. The middle phase was secret whereas the first and last phases were communal. At the end, each person became adult community participants. But the colonial government and the Christian Churches attacked the rite through indifference and aggressive support of the western-style educational system that we have now."

"I know that our Church was against these practices. I read about it in the archives."

"Yes the Churches were all against circumcision or initiation, polygamy and witchcraft. The Africans had to reconcile their Christian beliefs with their African roots. Western education has given us a degree of openness to European or Western ideas. But we must also keep our traditions if we are to help our fellow Basuto."

# Chapter Thirty

Both Veronica and Celeste passed their A-levels with distinction. Since Veronica had her elementary teacher's certificate already, she was asked if she would teach at the mission school in January. They agreed to give her room and board and pay her a small stipend. She agreed. Celeste was ecstatic.

"My father said that you could board with us and share my room. Isn't that great," Celeste exclaimed. "What are your future plans?" she asked Veronica.

"I am not sure. I have to write to Johnna in Canada. She is still at nursing School. But Johnna has a scholarship for me in Canada."

"Maybe while you are staying here you could convince my father to let me come with you!" Celeste said.

"Now, there's an idea!"

Veronica, in her letter to Johnna, asked if it were possible to find a scholarship for Celeste also. By return post both girls were advised of an appointment they had at the High Commission of Canada in Pretoria early in January.

When Veronica gave Celeste the news she was overjoyed. Celeste's mother was very instrumental in convincing the reverend Thomas Nkosi that he should stop being a doubting Thomas and let Celeste bring honour upon their family. Reluctantly he acquiesced.

The day spent in Pretoria at the High Commission was also rewarding. Both girls had received a scholarship to study Education at Simon Fraser University, in Vancouver, B.C. The High Commissioner who had known Johnna in Zambia took a special interest in these girls. From his own pocket he gave them spending money for their stop-overs in London and in Toronto. He had also telegraphed Johnna in Toronto with the good news and the date of their arrival in Toronto.

Johnna was overwhelmed by his generosity and immediately sent her thanks by telegram to Pretoria. Then she sat down to write to Veronica.

*Toronto, Ontario,*
*January, 1965.*

Dear Ma Paseka,

*God be praised! In a few months I will see you again. How happy I am for both of you! It will be nice that you are not alone. You will love the West Coast. The temperature is mild compared to other parts of Canada. You may even be able to visit Francina who is in Los Angeles. It seems that Celeste has the same dreams as you do. I await both of you eagerly in August when you arrive from London.*

*Keep well,*
*Your friend as always,*
*Johnna.*

When Veronica showed the letter that her brother Joseph had given her upon their arrival in Soweto, Celeste welled up with tears.

She had never seen so much care and concern from the Europeans. She had been taught that she couldn't expect that except within the PEMS group. She said to Veronica,

"I once was blind and now I see."

Back at Morija, Veronica taught and Celeste worked at the Printing Shop. Their days were full but in their room at night they chatted. They shared ideas and dreams. They melded a friendship that would last a long time.

When they left Morija, in mid-August for a last visit to Joseph in Soweto, Celeste felt that she was embarking on an odyssey, a great adventure. Though she was only two years younger than Veronica, her experiences left her always in awe. It also left her vulnerable. She was not by nature brave, but she knew that in Veronica's shadow she would learn and become strong.

Because they embraced the same ideals their bond was like the strands of a rope. Their strength came from their intertwining ideas. They culled many of their ideas from the African Feminist Thinkers to which they subscribed and their avid reading.

They arrived in Toronto in mid-August 1965.

Johnna had so much fun watching the reactions of these girls. She said,

"Welcome to my village!"

Since her apartment was too small, she had asked Luke if he would put the three of them up for few days. From there they toured Toronto, Ottawa, etc. In the evenings there were barbecues and get-togethers. Alan was always at these supper parties. When Veronica got Johnna alone she queried her relationship with him.

"Oh, Alan. He's from our home town and we all went to school together."

"He seems to keep close to you, Mè"

"He doesn't know all Luke's friends," she lied. "Now tell me about you and Celeste. Is it a serious liaison, like sexual maybe?"

Veronica laughed, "Heavens, no! We are wedded in spirit and aim. Both of us have been fiancéed but have deeper needs and are dedicated to bringing hope to the Basuto amid dire poverty and deepening despair. Our aim is to let education both formal and personal, build our resources so that we will be equipped to help people at the grassroots level in Basutoland. Everything we do is to that end. Can I continue to count on you to help me spiritually and financially? You remember what you told me about why, you are white and I am black."

"Yes of course I remember."

"Well I have elevated that paradigm to C to the fourth degree or $C^4$. Circumstance (happen to be there); Cultural a (Masotho); Colour –(black and white); and C – currency (financial help)."

"How clever you are! Yes, you can count on me for the fourth "C"!

"Mè, you remember how I wanted to become Catholic at one point at St. Joseph's? Being at Morija made me realize how belonging to one religion alienates one from people of other religions. Most religions strengthen the theological and spiritual life of its adherents while often neglecting the economic and social deprivation they endure. Thus the Good News of the Gospel is bad news if you are hungry and struggling to survive."

"True, Veronica, but Christ said, "The poor you'll always have with you," which meant that's the way it is. Our work is to alleviate their pain and to lessen it. We must continuously work to find balance in all things, thus harmony and peace. At my first lesson in philosophy the professor said, "Virtutes est in medio." Virtue lies in the middle." But your philosophy has merit."

Veronica and Celeste were eager and reluctant at the same time. They were eager to start their Bachelor of Education studies in Vancouver but were reluctant to leave Johnna.

To put their minds at ease, Johnna said as they awaited their flight at Pearson Airport,

"Remember, whatever you have your attention centered on is what you will create in your physical world. And don't worry about what you will do after Simon Fraser. "When the student is ready, the teacher will come." Go in peace, my dears."

She hugged each of them and as she did she left them each an envelope with "C⁴" for the trip.

In June 1969, two radiant Africa graduates received their Bachelor of Arts degree, "cum laude" (with honours).

From September 1970 to June 1972, Celeste and Veronica studied at St. Francis Xavier University in Antagonish, N.S. where they received a Master's Degree in Co-Op Management. They had learned how to set up village co-op's in a Third World Environment. The system was long in theory but slow in action and development.

Arriving back on South African soil after seven years was a shock even to them. That first evening at Joseph's in Soweto was an eye-opener for them.

"Last year the Black Homelands Citizenship Bill authorized the South African Government to withdraw citizenship for all Africans. We are all citizens of our Homelands. If you have no papers to prove that you can be here you will be endorsed out to your homeland."

"What does it mean, Joseph?" asked Veronica.

"It means that apartheid is getting crueller and crueller towards blacks. You both will do well by going to Lesotho to work."

"We intend to, Joseph. We have been given money to start working at the village level to set up a system called co-ops. We will rent a house to live in and another for our headquarters in Maseru. I also have a job teaching Religious Education at the University of Botswana, Lesotho and Swaziland in Roma."

# Chapter Thirty-One

By the time the second term began in August 1972, at the University, and Veronica was teaching there, the Lesotho Co-op Corporation had been licensed and the government had approved.

"The first thing we have to do is make out a three year, long-range plan of work. We have to decide where to start." said Veronica to her business associate, Celeste Nkosi.

Looking at a wall map of Lesotho she put a big X on Butha-Buthe and Mokhotlong, Thaba-Tseka and Qacha's Nek.

"These areas are too mountainous and some of the villages are only accessible by air. We cannot yet afford these expenses, so we will not include them in our first three-year plan." said Veronica.

"That makes good business sense, Mrs. Chairwoman." said Celeste.

"Thank you, Madame Secretary-Bursar," replied Veronica, as they both laughed.

Although both ladies could drive and had their licences, they had to hire a driver. It was wise to always have a man when visiting distant villages. They knew the customs and the ordinary Masoto (singular Basuto) was still steeped in traditions, especially where women were concerned. And so it was that Moeletsi was hired.

When Veronica interviewed him she said,

"Your name is appropriate, I believe it means "Adviser" and we will depend on your advice especially with regard to our vehicle, which is a VW mini-bus. And your English is very good. We will let you know tomorrow.

When she spoke with Celeste, she said,

"He is married so he will be stable. He has a family to feed and needs the job. What do you say?"

"Whatever you decide."

"No, no, Celeste. You must be a partner, not a yes-person. If it doesn't work out and you expressed your opinion, then you can say to me, I told you so!"

"Well, I checked him out in his village and I was told he is not a joala (beer) drinker. So I say, let's hire him."

"For the next few weeks, Celeste made lists of the districts they would visit and the names of the villages in each district. She went to the government library as well as the local library. Veronica got involved in her teaching at the university and the two met for the evening meal. Slowly, slowly they built up their plan. Veronica realized that she could not do justice to both jobs, so at the end of term in November 1972 she resigned her teaching post and did co-op work full time.

They set up study clubs in each village they visited. They explained what co-op meant—it was to increase their standard of living by sharing the production and the consumption of their productivity. At first, the chiefs were hostile, they wanted to take over the co-op once it was working and producing. They found leaders in each village who understood the concept. They explained to the people that it was another way of making decisions that affected their lives directly without depending on the political professionals to dole out assistance. They would be stronger if they organized themselves horizontally in their struggle against poverty and deprivation. Once the production of food was shared they understood the principle.

The next step was production to sell and then share the profits. The co-op would become an outlet for household woven goods and cottage industries particular to the Basuto items made from grass, like hats, baskets and clay items. Soon they had to find wider markets. Celeste suggested that they sell items to tourists or to shops who sold them to tourists. Slowly, slowly the co-op grew. Some villages were more successful than others depending on leaders. In the third year they had established themselves in all but four of the ten districts. They had increased their staff, their vehicles, their drivers. Their non-denominational status was major to their success. Yet both ladies felt a gnawing at their heartstring to move on. They found a leader who could take over as Chairman and there were others from whom other functionnaires could be chosen.

So after four years they handed over the reigns. The organization now did not need overseas funding; they had become self-reliant.

Veronica and Celeste's careers took off on different tangents but they kept in loose contact as they set out on the next phase of helping their fellow Basotho living outside of Basutoland. Teaching them and guiding them out of their misery and oppression became their aim.

Veronica moved back to Seweto, in a room her brother Joseph rented to her. He had a growing family and the money was dearly needed. After Johnna lost her husband Alan, she inherited her second fortune. She sent a bi-yearly donation to Veronica so she could continue her work. It was a very generous amount which Veronica put to good use and shared with her dear friend Celeste.

# Chapter Thirty-Two

From her small room in Joseph's home in Soweto in 1976, Veronica began another phase of a life lived for her Basuto brothers and sisters.

She started by joining Steve Biko's group of SA Students' Organization as a counsellor. Through SASO she was able to meet other anti-apartheid or resistance groups.

She coached the sports in her area thus empowering the youth through sports. She realized that the future leaders were thus being trained by the determination and discipline demanded to excel.

In a letter to Johnna at that time, Veronica wrote:

"I was not aware of the deep conflicts that had developed between the Whites and the Africans. I had been educated by whites in the mission schools and while in Canada received an education with white professors who were liberal and sympathetic to our cause in South Africa. I had no real difficulty with the idea of cooperation between blacks and whites when I thought of whites such as those. Now however, as you used to say, "That's a different bag of beans!" My work now is so militant like Francina's, but my methods and ideologies are different. I am an activist for the liberation of the blacks, particularly my own Basuto Tribe but my tools are to educate, to illuminate and help them eradicate fear and restore their self-esteem. It is the first step to freedom."

Her first real break came when she joined an ecumenical organization Koinonia, working for social justice and racial reforms. It was an offshoot of "Learn Together", which brought together whites and blacks. On week nights they met in church halls and were led by a sympathetic dominee (minister of the Dutch Reform Church-SA) by means of books, presentations and discussions, all the members shared their experiences and knowledge.

On this particular night, two assignments were handed out. Wilhelm Van Horne was assigned to make a presentation on "Dr. Christiaan Frederick Beyers Naudé." And Veronica was given the task to make a presentation on "Ubuntu—an African Religious Philosophy."

She said to Wilhelm,

"I know why I have been given this assignment but I don't know why you have been given yours."

Wilhelm in his mid-thirties with an easy smile said, "I received a Master's Degree in Theology from Stellenbosch University where Dr. Beyers Naudé was a professor. We became good friends. I returned under his guidance to study at the Christian Institute which he had founded in 1963. It was here that I learned about Liberation Theology and inter-faith activities."

"That is powerful. I am eager to hear your exposé." she said.

Veronica was the first to deliver her paper. She started off;

"Fellow Activists:
We inhabit the same country but live in totally different worlds. Neutrality with regard to the conflict that is raging in South Africa today is an illusion. Our group is building solidarity in the struggle. Something new is groaning to emerge. Preaching the Gospel in South Africa today is closely bound up with its social, political, and economic history. The Gospel, by both the British and the Afrikaners was justified and legitimized by colonialism, imperialism and European superiority. By barbaric methods and attitudes, colonizers firmly believe that what they were bringing to this part of the world was "civilization" and the basis of that civilization was the message of Jesus Christ.

The original preachers of the gospel in South Africa were: first the chaplains and the ministers who came to preach and minister to the colonial officials, soldiers and settlers. And secondly, the various missioners who came to evangelize the indigenous and colonize Africa. They had divided traditions, these denominations that came; the Anglicans, the Methodists, the Congregationalists, the Presbyterians, the Baptists and the Catholics were mostly involved in medical and educational needs but not in social justice."

The Dutch Reformed Church of Calvinist heritage known simply as the DRC has now developed into the Christian National Doctrine and became deeply involved in the politics, economy, and social life of the Afrikaner. They declared that apartheid was in accordance with Scripture and that ethnic purity was the divine will. This led to the need for racial separation.

The white Church became the Settlers Church and the black Church became the Missionary Church. Seventy-eight per cent of South Africans identify themselves as Christian. Of these eighty-eight per cent are black. But which God do we follow? Our God or their God? Which Gospel is Christ's message? Their Gospel or our Gospel? What South Africa needs today is a new-look at the African philosophy and way of life called, "Ubuntu." It is a Zulu word meaning humanness. Western humanism denies the importance of religious beliefs whereas African humanism has traditionally, a deeply religious meaning, whoever the Supreme Being may be.

The concept of Ubuntu means the respect for others, using the same criteria for judging the other and finally a mutual exposure through inter-religious dialogue.

Ubuntu may in the future help South Africa forget and forgive once justice is restored, the blacks are released from poverty and a decent life is attainable. It may help the "oppressed" not to turn the tables and it may help the "oppressor" to re-discover a common humanity.

Thank you!"

The clapping was long and sincere. Wilhelm approached her and said: "I've spoken about you to Dr. Naudé and he wishes to meet you. As you know he is under house arrest and can only meet with two people at a time. When you and I go there, his wife will leave for a shopping spree so the police surveillance will not interrupt us because we will only be two."

"Really? The surveillance is that strict?"

"Yes, he can only meet with two people at a time, whether in his home or anywhere within his area of designated confinement. The system (as the Government is called) is very paranoid."

At the next meeting, Wilhelm gave his presentation to the group.

"Good evening!
I could enumerate several statistics about Dr. Beyers Naudé to point out how he became a man of conscience when as Saint Paul, he was knocked off his horse. Until 1960 the practice and preached racial segregation, adhered to the tenets of the Broederbond and the Dutch Reformed Church.

He believed in ethnic purity, in ethnic destiny and separate development as his forefathers had. But after the Sharpeville Massacres of 1960 when government troops shot sixty-nine unarmed youth demonstrators, he aligned himself with the World Council of Churches to condemn apartheid. In 1961, he founded the Christian Institute as an ecumenical organization. But it soon became drawn into the Liberation Movement.

In 1973, he was convicted of a technical offense against the government's Suppression of Communism Act and was subsequently made officially voiceless and forbidden to comment on public issues in South Africa by being banned. He was kept under constant police surveillance by plainclothesmen who parked their cars or vans opposite his home in a suburb of Johannesburg, which he shares with his wife. He may not move outside of a prescribed area of the city and is forbidden to speak to more that two people at a time, even in the privacy of his home.

The Christian Institute is interdenominational, interracial organization that maintains that the "gospel of apartheid" was false. He declared that the Bible conveyed clearly that God created all nations of the world in one blood, creating the unity of the human race. In 1977 Naudé and the C.I. were banned. He was defrocked from the DRC for inter-faith activities and joined the African Reformed Church. This is truly a man of conscience.

Thank you."

Veronica clapped louder than most. She said to Wilhelm,

"You were brilliant. I am very eager to meet this man. When are we going there?"

"Tonight at eight o'clock. I'll pick you up at your place at seven. Is that ok?"

"That is just perfect. I have been thinking about this meeting for several days. Some directives I need about my future work."

"Good. See you then."

The house in Hillbrow was very plain. Veronica had never seen so many books in a private home before. She felt at home in this man's presence immediately. He had an aura of wisdom and peace about him. His lovely wife had excused herself after our meeting to leave just two other people with Dr. Naudé as the government ban required.

"Now Veronica," he said, "Wilhelm has told me about you. He also told me you need direction on how to channel your talents to help in the liberation of the South African blacks, particularly at this time.

I read in the paper this morning that Steve Biko has died in police custody. He will be buried outside King William's town in the Eastern Cape, near his family home. It is a big loss for our movement."

"Yes," replied Veronica. "It is a big loss for our cause. He was so ardent."

"Now my dear, we have so little time together. We had better get started."

"Very well," said Veronica. "To save time I wrote a resumé of my education and co-op work in Lesotho. When the co-op became viable, we left a very successful enterprise in the hands of the Basuto themselves in Lesotho. But there are more Basuto outside Lesotho than in, so I came back to Soweto to dedicate myself to the cause. I joined several students' organizations, worked with youth groups in Soweto. But my comfort zone hit a high when I joined the ecumenical organization. Through them I realized how-deep the hatred of the blacks for the whites ran. Then I came across a quote from Robert Sobukwe who no longer believed in pacificism. He said, "Every time our people have shown signs of uniting against oppression, their white friends have come along and broken that unity… The white missionaries have done the same thing… Our people now hate the white man because they associate him with oppression. If you remove the association, you remove the hatred."

I had a friend in the Junior Certificate course in Khukhune, Lesotho who was a staunch freedom fighter even at school. I envied her deep conviction but could not endorse the way Francina has become a Freedom Fighter and as far as I know she's still going strong. So I am trying to find my niche and I need your guidance, doctor."

"Veronica, I can only recommend a path to you. You must follow your own destiny. As you know, the Christian Institute has been banned. I have been banned from the DRC, the Broederbond and all things government. But we have kept our spirit and since I joined the African Dutch Reformed Church more avenues have opened up to our Liberation Theology Institute. We are preparing a document that will be published and distributed world wide. I hope to present it to the World Council of Churches in Geneva. Because it is such an important anti-apartheid tool we must be sure that our research and presentation are accurate.

Each Christian concept must be presented in the light of liberation of the South African blacks.

Such concepts will be studied, researched historically, biblically, etc, and then printed up into a unified document. We have decided to call it the "Kairos Document." Kairos meaning "the moment of divine grace," as in Galatians 4:4–5. "When the fullness of time has come, God sent forth his Son ... to redeem them that were under the law, that we might receive the adoption of sons.""

"It sounds like a monumental document. And which facet have you assigned to me?"

"You and Wilhelm will collaborate on the Justice and Peace section. Wilhelm will be able to set up conferences and student study groups for you at the universities. He will be your constant companion and act as a body guard. He will also act as liaison with me since it is easier for him to come to me. There is just one requirement and that is that you are willing to die for the cause of liberation of your fellow Africans. Can you accept that?"

"Yes, with all my heart, I can, Sir."

On their way back to Soweto Veronica said to Wilhelm,

"I am so happy to be working with you. You instil confidence in me and my dreams. You help me to see things that I was really protected from. When I was in my early twenties I fell in love and was asked in marriage. But there was a little gnawing voice that kept saying, "You have a higher destiny." I battled with the demons until, one of my teachers, a Catholic Sister from Canada quoted the poet Khalil Gibran who said, "When you are born, your work is placed in your heart." Then I knew I had to deny my human love for a run at my dream."

"You flatter me, Veronica. I am the one who is honoured to be working with you. That "dream" of yours? Once you let it turn into a dream, it won't ever happen for you. So don't let it turn into a dream. It is your life work."

"You are so wise Wilhelm," Veronica said, as their eyes met, on her way to the first day of the rest of her life.

# Chapter Thirty-Three

In 1978, Veronica had met Dr. Beyers Naudé and was given her assignment on Justice and Peace in collaboration with Wilhelm Van Horne. It was also the year Robert Sobokwe died. It was a great loss for the resistance movement as he was an inspiration and a true prophet.

Veronica and Wilhelm were deeply involved on the Working Committee for the Kairos Document. Participants met monthly for plenary meetings of various committees. The cultural conflict was expressed in terms of race; the economic development was studied with the massive oppression; the political domination was measured against the resistance groups and finally the military power versus guerilla tactics.

As the months and years went on, Wilhelm became enamored with Veronica. Then one evening he declared his love for her. She had known for a long time now and had been extremely careful not to encourage it.

She said to him,

"Wilhelm I love you and being with you is most enjoyable. I have had visions of our having a life together but it is only a dream and will never be, as you once said to me. We cannot be accused of aiming too low. We cannot be responsible for letting our personal life subtract from the good of the poor for whom we are dedicated. I am flattered and grateful. I think our sacrifice will bring justice for them and bring peace to each of us."

Wilhelm was deeply shaken. He took both her hands in his and said,

"I can only love our God more than you. And strangely, I love you more now than I ever did and I always will. Thank you."

They got on with their lives and basically were inseparable.

In July, 1985 the first state of emergency was proclaimed in the Townships. Many were killed, injured, maimed for life or thrown into lock-ups. On September 25$^{th}$, the Kairos Document was published. On the following day, Veronica and Wilhelm had a meeting with a students' group at Stellenbosch University. They met briefly with Dr. Naudé. He proudly gave Veronica a thank you hug and shook hands with Wilhelm. He blessed them as he sent them on their way.

Wilhelm set up microphones, the slide projector, charts, etc. Veronica began,

"This year more than twenty people were killed by police in Langa Township of Cape Town. Violence has escalated in many other townships. The government has declared a state of emergency and become more brutal"

Wilhelm showed slides of the chaos in the townships.

Veronica continued,

"The state of continued violence makes individual non-violence impossible. The only hope to prevent the oppression is violence. It is justice against tyranny and is justified. In our long Christian traditions in our churches we prayed for good government. But we will have to pray for the conversion to truth of the Dutch Reformed Church itself, to have good government. The State Theology legitimizes state-sponsored violence by providing divine legitimacy to the State. The Church theology, by ignoring the socio-economic and political injustice unwittingly supports those in power. We represent a prophetic theology and we will distribute our document to you so that we can discuss it. You will need courage to speak of things as they are and that will give you hope to see the way forward so that South Africa might be changed and all her people may have freedom from want and freedom from fear. It will be a long and arduous process because those who have more than enough are often unwilling to do what it takes to meet the needs of those who have less than sufficient."

Wilhelm, with the help of some students began distributing the documents. Meanwhile Veronica was surrounded by eager students asking her questions.

Suddenly she fell to the floor. Wilhelm ran to her. She looked up at him with a smile on her face and said,

"You'll have to work twice as hard now but with my eternal love as your new partner."

She turned her head and died.

One of the students pointed to a sniper, picking up his scope as he turned to flee. They all knew that "the system" was responsible.

Wilhelm contacted Celeste Nkosi after the body was brought to Joseph's in Soweto. Celeste knew what she had to do. They had discussed both eventuality of it happened to either of them

She wrote to Johnna.

*26 September, 1985.*

*Dear Mrs. Forrest,*

*I am the bearer of sad news. Veronica was giving a presentation to launch the "Kairos Document" that she and Wilhelm Van Horne have been working on for years. Wilhelm assures me that she mailed you a copy. While he was distributing copies to the students, Veronica was answering student questions privately when a sniper bullet pierced her heart. She lived a few minutes to pass the torch on to Wilhelm as he held her.*

*Her ashes will be taken to Morija for burial as she had planned. When we spoke of this eventuality she told me to write to you and tell you that she has now five C's.*

*1) Circumstances,*
*2) Colour,*
*3) Culture,*
*4) Currency,*
*5) Cherub.*

*She added in her joking way that God willing the second C would be white at last.*

*White at last. She added that you would understand fully.*

*I await your response about how to finalize her finances, etc.*

*Yours sincerely,*
*Celeste Nkosi*

# PART FIVE
## "THE LADIES"

All "The Ladies" meet in Pretoria,
South Africa to bury Veronica, who has been killed by
a sniper bullet at a student rally at the university.

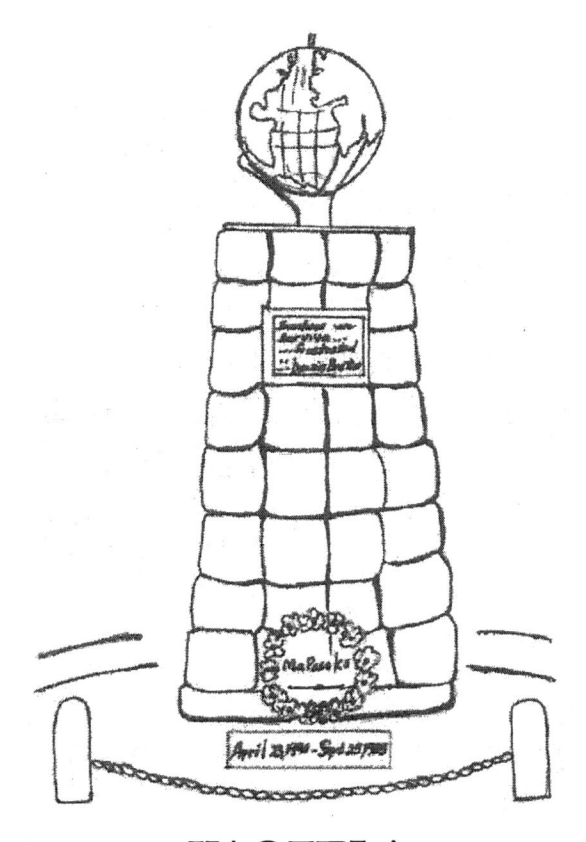

## KAOFELA
### (Everyone)

# Chapter Thirty-Four
## "The Ladies"

Johnna read Celeste Nkosi's letter dated the 26th September, 1985 about Veronica's death. Her tears were uncontrollable at the thought of this beautiful friend gunned down for trying to liberate the downtrodden in her own native land. Shot down by a fellow countryman? In the army they would call that friendly fire. But in South Africa they call it protecting the nation against communism and black liberation.

Mora came down for breakfast and was upset by his mother's tears. He had never seen her cry.

"Mother, what's the matter?"

"Oh Mora! Our dear Veronica has been shot by a sniper at a presentation she was giving at Stellenbosch University."

"Shot?"

"Yes darling, shot!"

Just then Suzanne Smith, who had been living with the Forrests since Mara was in her Montessori class twenty years ago, came upon the sad situation.

Johnna explained why she was so devastated.

"Oh! I'm sorry. It's so far. There's no way you can go for the burial."

"No, but I have plans for a memorial for the "Bo-Mè" that is "The Ladies" in Pretoria. So her ashes will be buried in Lesotho and then, when we are able we will transfer her remains. Mora and I have planned this memorial for several years now, not for anyone of us in particular but for all of us eventually. When the political climate allows us to go ahead with our plans. I must write to Celeste and explain everything to her, about Veronica's chattel, etc.

In her letter she explained how the remaining funds were to be distributed. Johnna knew approximately how much money was in the account since she sent it to her each month.

Joseph would inherit her worldly goods including the car. Celeste and Wilhelm would take her books, files, etc, and her personal effects. Her ashes are to be kept in an urn in Morija, Lesotho, to be eventually transferred to their common memorial in Pretoria some day.

The money is to be distributed thus; one-quarter each to Joseph and Celeste and one-half to Wilhelm to continue Veronica and Wilhelm's work. It was a goodly sum.

In 1994, Mora, while still at the University, marries his sweetheart also a student. They are both studying law. At twenty-one, Mora began receiving his yearly trust allowance that Johnna had set up for him soon after Alan's death. Johnna and Suzanne found themselves alone. Both of them had retired at sixty and traveled a lot since then.

Their first overseas trip, however, in March of 1996, was to Italy. Suzanne had taken over Mora's part in the development and assembly of the "Bo-Mè Memorial." They went to Rome to have the memorial commissioned for sculpturing. The artists would come to Pretoria to set it up and be ready by the time they transferred Veronica's ashes in mid-June. Johnna and Suzanne spent four weeks in Rome seeing to the work they had commissioned and visiting all that Rome had to offer.

Before Johnna and Suzanne left Rome for South Africa, they made one final visit to the sculptor's. Johnna was ecstatic with the work. She paid half of the grand total, which included return airfares for four workers to travel to Pretoria to complete the work. They would receive the other half when the work was completed by the 15th of June. The arrangements were accepted and the contract signed to everyone's satisfaction.

# Chapter Thirty-Five

On April 20th, 1996 the two women arrived at Jan Smuts Airport in the early afternoon. Maria DeKock, Johnna's friend of many years, was there with her husband to meet them. They stayed with them in Johnnesburg. During that time, Johnna purchased a Nissan van so the remaining "Bo-Mè" could travel to visit St. Joseph's at Khukhune and on to Morija in the south to collect the urn with Veronica's ashes.

On May 2nd, Johnna drove the Nissan to Celeste's in Soweto. She knocked on the door of Celeste's. The children gathered around the new van which was a rarity in the poverty-stricken township.

When Celeste opened the door she exclaimed,

"Oh, Mrs. Forrest. How nice to meet you. Do come in, please."

When she and Suzanne walked into the small house, there was a tall white man in the living room. Johnna said,

"Hello. You must be Wilhelm. I have heard so much about you over the years. And congratulations on your marriage. How many years has it been now?

"Since the laws that prohibited interracial marriage in 1978, were repealed in 1986, which allowed Celeste and I to marry. So we were free to get married then. We still had a problem living together. But since Nelson Mandela became President we were free in this area also. So we have kept both residences since it helps us in our work. My home in Hillbrow is used mainly for meetings, etc. Also our work now is getting help for the poor, helping the AIDS victims, etc, along with our work with Dr. Naudé's Christian Institute. But I am being carried away here."

Celeste interjected,

"And this must be Miss Smith?"

"Oh! Heavens, Celeste, I am sorry, this is Suzanne Smith my live-in companion. And please call me Johnna."

After spending an afternoon getting acquainted Johnna explained her plans.

"Wilhelm, on May 14th when the "Bo-Mè" as we have called ourselves, since 1962, want to visit Khukhune, and Morija, Lesotho.

We would like to hire you as our driver for that trip. And Celeste we want you to come along. Is that possible?"

"Celeste dear, get our schedule so we can check the dates. You say May 14th until which date, Johnna?"

"May 14th to the 30th."

They checked their appointments and decided that with a few slight adjustments, they could be available.

"Oh, great! We are staying at the Hilton in Johannesburg until May 6th. So that gives us three days to be with you. We will leave it up to you about how we can visit Stellenbosch University where Veronica was gunned down. I want to visit your headquarters at the Christian Institute and if possible meet Dr. Naudè. Is that too ambitious, Wilhelm?"

"No, all that can be arranged. Johnna, I haven't told anyone what Veronica's last words to me were. But I would like to share them with you. When we worked all those years together on the Kairos Document, I fell in love with her and when I proposed marriage she said, "Wilhelm, I love you dearly and being with you is most enjoyable. I have had visions of our having a life together but it is only a dream and will never be, as you once said to me." Then after she was shot and I held her in my arms, she said with a most beautiful smile on her face, "You'll have to work twice as hard now but with my eternal love as your new partner." I like to think that I have two partners now—her and Celeste."

Suzanne and Johnna left as planned on May 6th to visit the Van Zyl's in Pretoria. They would spend four days with the family.

"MaThusa!" exclaimed Eva as she opened the door to the visitors.

"MaDithaba, (Mother of Dreams), hello." Dumela said Johnna. This is my friend and companion Suzanne Smith."

"How do you do, Mè? I have heard all about you over the years and am pleased to finally meet you."

They entered a fine home in Pretoria's government employees district.

Piet Van Zyl now 54 was just beginning to turn gray. They met John who was twenty-six now. He was tall and very like his mother.

He was lighter in colour than she was but had slightly curly hair, more arabic-looking that the native peppercorn.

Piet was now Deputy Minister of Economic Development in the new government. He promised to take them for a visit to his ministry in two days. Because he knew that tomorrow, the women would spend the day reminiscing. And that, they did. Johnna told Eva of her plan for the memorial and for the "Bo-Mè's visit to Khukhune and Morija. Could she get time off from May 14 to May 30$^{th}$?

"Yes, yes, yes! I wouldn't miss that for anything," chirped Eva.

She was so excited. She said she would let Johnna and Suzanne visit the ministry with Piet while she made sure she could get the time off.

Piet was thrilled to travel to his ministry in the new van. After showing the ladies where the work of Economic Development was carried out, he brought them to his personal office.

"Most of our work is done via statistics. One of the most depressing facts for our economy today is the penury of Africans ready to move into posts vacated by whites who vacated downtown Johannesburg and took their money with them. In 1994, the government had had three years of negative growth, what you would call in Canada, a deficit. The economy and wealth of the nation is shrinking. We have had more than a decade of declining growth per capita. And the disproportionate allocations of educational resources to whites in the past has slowed the education of blacks. South Africa is in its 21$^{st}$ year of double-digit inflation. The inadequacies in housing, electricity, access to clean water, and sanitation are eating away at resources. Compounded with the Africans' general impatience with the new government, there has been an increase in gangsterism, drugs and HIV-Aids.

"Yes, I have kept abreast of the situation and it will be a long time before the government turns the corner and begins to see normalcy. We can only keep working and hoping. As Veronica used to say, "The rich get richer and the poor get poorer." We thank you for your wonderful, educational tour."

Too soon their visit with the Van Zyl's came to an end and they were on their way to spend a few days with Francina and family.

Daniel Makidisi was a tall, handsome African. He was Dean of African Languages at the English University of Johannesburg. When Johnna met him she said,

"I wish I had known you in the early sixties when I struggled to learn Sesotho."

He laughed and said,

"I was just fourteen then and being Xhosa knew very little Sesotho. But I did have a facility with languages even as Francina has."

"MaThuso!" Francina hugged her dear friend of thirty-four years.

She introduced Suzanne to them. And Francina quickly said they must find her an African name. She thought and thought and finally said,

"Keromang," which means "one who was sent", because you were sent to Johnna to be a companion in her older years."

"That's really fitting, Francina. I think I will probably just call her Kero for short."

They all laughed.

"And now for the pièce de resistance. Our son Khabane (The Warrior) just like his new ex-freedom fighter mom was. And the joy of our life Nyakallo (Joy)."

"Oh, they are beautiful Francina. Well worth the wait I am sure!"

As it was with Eva, the first day was spent reminiscing. Then Johnna told them of the plan to travel on May 14th to the 30th. They would visit Khukhune and Morija and bring back Veronica's ashes for burial at their common memorial on June 16th. That is the new Youth Day proclaimed by the Mr. Mandela's government.

"Would you be given time-off to make the trip, Francina?"

"No doubt. if Daniel doesn't mind caring for the children."

"I would be delighted. You may go with my blessing," replied Daniel.

In the next couple of days, Johnna and Suzanne visited the Ministry of Education in Pretoria, the English University in Johannesburg.

They returned to Wilhelm and Celeste's for final preparations. On the morning of the 14th, Eva and Francina arrived in Soweto.

When Francina read the name of the new Nissan she shouted,"The Quest! The Quest! The van is named after our club! The "Bo-Mè" continue their Quest in the Quest!"

"Francina, I stood at the back of the van when I was at your house but you didn't notice me point to the name. I made sure I had a Nissan Quest, blue in colour when I arrived in Johannesburg. I was in contact with Maria DeKock who, with her husband made sure it was ready for me when I arrived on April 20th."

Eva said,

"Mè, You never cease to astound us with your surprises and generosity."

"Eva, my dear, the circumstances in my life have given me an abundance. And remember the prayer of St. Francis we used to read at St. Joseph? Especially the part where it says, "It is in giving that we receive." I have experienced it over and over again, the more I give the more I get."

Wilhelm was the driver and Celeste sat in front with him. In the second row sat Francina, Johnna and Eva. Suzanne sat in the third row by herself.

Both Francina and Eva wanted to move back so she wouldn't be alone. Johnna, ever the teacher and the provider of surprises said to them,

"No, no. you stay put. God will provide. Trust him."

Wilhelm drove to the Hilton Hotel in Johannesburg and stopped at the front entrance. He gets out and spoke to the doorman. A few minutes later, an attractive, well-dressed woman came toward the van. Johnna and her two companions got out to let her into the back with Suzanne.

All of a sudden, all decorum abandoned, Francina and Eva shouted in unison,

"Basadi!(woman!) It's Ma Likatse! (The Mother of cats!) Sister Irene Kendall's Sesotho name that she was called by, in the early sixties at St. Joseph's, Khukhune."

What rejoicing! What a surprise! Once they were all settled, Wilhelm headed for northern Lesotho. They arrived at Khukhune at around 2 p.m. The old buildings were still there but they were not used as classrooms anymore.

Johnna, Francina and Eva went to the old rectory where their three years of JC has been spent. There was no life there now except the creatures which had full reign of the place all to themselves. Johnna went into her old bedroom off the classroom. Gingerly, she opened the old cupboard. What a surprise, her old billycan was still there, all covered in dust and cobwebs. She pulled it out and using a Kleenex, dusted it off and opened it. Her handwritten notes were still there especially the facts about the Quest Club members. She read the names: Eva Kukami; Francina Tsolo; Veronica Mohlana; Sister Emily. She kept the notes which she could complete once back in Canada with the living history of each after 30 plus years.

She left the billy-can and closed the old cupboard door. What memories rose up in her! There was no bitterness about them, they just were what they had been. That was then and this now, she thought. The group left after tea to arrive in Maseru before dark where they were booked for the night at the Lesotho Sun Hotel. Wilhelm and Celeste had their room. Francina and Eva had theirs and the three older women shared one.

The next morning they drove to the airport where they boarded a plane for Mokhotlong in the mountains. They were all bundled up in warm clothes because winter had begun. And at 6998 metres a.s.l. it would be cold. They were booked into the Lefu Hotel, five kilometres from the airfield. Once they were established in their respective rooms, they met in the small dining area. They rented a mini-bus cum driver and made their first foray into the awesome mountains. They stopped at a tourists' look-out. From there, they saw the majestic Drakensburg Mountains often the called Switzerland of Africa. It was also known locally as the "Roof of Africa." To the south-east the Thabana-Ntlenyana at 3482 m. rose its majestic head. The Basuto called it the Littlest Mountain; the irony of its claim as the highest point in Southern Africa. Everyone whispered the remarks they shared as though in presence of the divine as though having come full circle, Johnna said out loud to Irene, like she did in the early sixties,

"Wow!"

The next day they took a pony trek of two hours each way to see some local falls on the great Orange River. The trek had left all of them stiff in the hind quarters so they spent the next day just lazing in the cold sunshine. It was an adventure they would never forget. They flew back to Maseru where they spent the night, before the drive to Morija.

At Morija they were received by Celeste's parents. Thomas her father, was now retired from teaching and the ministry. They lived in a mud hut furnished by Paris Evangelical Mission Society. It was large and quite comfortable but mud nevertheless.

Johnna took Celeste aside and said to her,

"Find out what it would cost to build them a frame house and I will give you a cheque to pay for it."

Celeste stood dumbfound and didn't move. She looked as though she was having a seizure of some kind.

"Yoo-hoo!" said Johnna, "Are you alright?"

"Why would you do that for us?"

"Because I can. Call it a gift in honour of our dear friend Veronica's memory."

When Celeste told her father, big tears welled-up in his now rheumy eyes and he said,

"Mè, you are an epiphany of Christ. You shall be in my daily prayers. My wife and I are most grateful."

"Now now, Reverend Nkosi. That's the Lord's way of rewarding you on this earth for your devotion and service to others. Please just thank Him. I am only a channel of His."

On June 14th, they returned to Pretoria via Bloemfontein in the Orange Free state. They had Veronica with them now, the "Bo-Mè" were complete again. They began to recite Dennis Brutus's poem learned so many years ago.

Johnna announced the title as she did way back then;

"Somehow We Survive."

The three of them continued with deep reverence:

*"Somehow we survive*
*and tenderness, frustrated, does not wither.*
*Investigating searchlights rake*
*our naked unprotected contours;*

*over our heads the monolithic Decalogue*
*of fascist prohibition glowers*
*and teeters for a catastrophic fall;*
*boots club the peeling door.*
*But somehow we survive*
*severance, deprivation, loss.*
*Patrols uncoil along the asphalt dark*
*hissing their menace to our lives,*
*most cruel, all our land is scarred with terror,*
*rendered unlovely and unlovable;*
*sundered are we and all our passionate surrender*
*but somehow tenderness survives.'*
                                                    *—Dennis Brutus.*

A dramatic silence followed.

# Chapter Thirty-Six

Back at the Johannesburg Hilton, Irene said to Johnna, "What will you be doing between the first of June and the fifteenth?"

"Knowing Johnna, as I do, I am sure she had it all planned," interjected Suzanne.

"You are right ladies. These two weeks are for us "bakoa" (white ones). We are going to see the wildlife in Kruger National park for seven days."

"And? And? What about the other seven days? asked Irene.

"We will visit Sun City before heading back Johannesburg on the 14th. Casino, theatre, dining, even a zoo!" Fun! Fun!"

"I told you she had it all planned. And I am sure all the reservations have been made too." said Suzanne.

"I booked everything in Canada with Thomas Cook Travel. It was cheaper to pay in Canadian dollars."

They took a taxi to the airport where they were booked for a flight to Durban. The next morning after breakfast, they began their journey by super bus along the Natal North coast towards Zululand. They checked in at the Simunye Zulu lodge. This experience began with an ox-cart transfer to the lodge. The activities at the lodge were varied and interesting. At the lodge they experienced the fascinating cross-cultural influences that have emerged since Zulu and Western culture first interacted in pioneer days. After dinner, they sat mesmerized around the fire as the Zulu legends unfolded to the rhythmic drumbeat of Africa. After a restful sleep, the bus left for the famous Timbavati Private Nature reserve part of the Great Kruger National Park. They spent two nights at Kings Camp. Their game viewing was excellent. They saw elephants, wild buffalo, lions, rhinos, leopards and many gazelles of various kinds. From there the bus brought them back to Johannesburg.

Johnna visited the site in Pretoria. This was June 12th and the work was nearly complete. The three ladies couldn't believe how beautiful it was. Johnna asked the sculptor to come to the Hilton to sign the papers and receive his final cheque that afternoon. She had

Maria DeKock's husband draw-up all the papers etc. That afternoon everything was finalized.

The masons would be there on the fifteenth to cement in Veronica's urn with a plaque as in the contract.

"Still three days, Johnna. What have you organized?" asked Irene.

"We are taking a three day bus tour to Sun City. There, we will have fun gambling, watch a couple of first class shows. I believe "Cats" is one of them. Then we come back on the fifteenth."

It was Irene this time who said, "Wow."

The 16$^{th}$ of July, 1996, was a bright cool day. The sun shone incandescent through the early morning fog caused by a thousand fires from the township rather than a high humidity. It was so typically African. At ten in the morning the remaining Bo-Mè and all the invitees gathered at the Freedom Cemetery in Pretoria. The memorial was surrounded by small square white pillars from which large black chains encircled the area. There was one entry along a pink marble walk that led to the centre monolith of alabaster. Upon the first side of the pillar was a large bronze plaque upon which was engraved in relief the following epitaph:

> Veronica, MaPaseka, Mohlana
> April 23, 1940 – September 25, 1985
> Born in Soweto, South Africa.
> Was gunned down by a sniper bullet trying
> to free her people from oppressive bondage,
> at Stellenbosch University.
> "The bird does not sing because it has to
> but because it has a song."

Minister Nkosi from Morija said the prayers and Wilhelm placed the urn into the receptacle built into the side of the pillar.

Then the testimonials began with Johnna,

"On September 25, 1985 in a holy instant, Veronica went from now-here to no-where. But it was not the end. The divine, changeless, invisible Veronica will live on. Her sacred self was never born and will never die."

Then Wilhelm picked up,

"Any man's death diminishes me because I am involved in mankind; and therefore never send to know for whom the bell tolls; it tolls for thee by John Donne (1572–1631)".

After all the testimonials had been given, Wilhelm, Celeste, Suzanne, Irene, Francina and Eva remained behind to admire the memorial that they had not had time to explore. They walked around silently. On the other three sides of the pillar, were the remaining names etched on a bronze plate.

Johnna Rymhs, Forrest, a.k.a. MaThuso,
Francina Tsolo, Makidisi, a.k.a. MaMofirifiri,
Eva, Kukami, Van Zyl, a.k.a. MaDithaba,

Also there was a receptacle for future urns on each of the remaining three sides of the pillar. On the top of the pillar was a globe of the world made of blue marble, with land masses of green, with four hands reaching across it; one pink and three brown. Between the four hands was etched "Bo-Mè". Etched in black bas-relief on the pink walkway surrounding the pillar was their favourite poem. At the entrance, on the first pink marble walk was etched:

"Somehow We Survive"
–Dennis Brutus

Four consecutive lines on each of the four sides of the pillar were etched in the pink marble, completing the entire poem around the pillar. The seven friends silently walked around marveling at Johnna's forethought and ingenuity.

Finally, the three Canadian ladies were ready to leave. It was arranged that Francina and her family, Eva and her family, Wilhelm and Celeste would come to see them off at Jan Smuts Airport. The evening before, Johnna has gone with Wilhelm to say good bye to Veronica's brother Joseph who was now very frail. On the way back to Johannesburg, Johnna gave a large manila envelope to Wilhelm saying,

"These are the transfer of ownership insurance, etc. for the Quest van. I want to feel that I am with you, Celeste and Veronica in all your work especially for HIV-Aids."

The goodbyes at the airport were heart wretching for all. The South Africans thought, those ladies will always help us in our ever continuing Quest!

"Mayi buje I Africa! ("Let Africa return") they chanted.

# Glossary

**ablutions:** These were carried out in one's room as the only tub was in the main building. Hot water was heated on the kitchen stove and carried to the bathroom. Pitchers of hot water were brought to the rooms every evening for ablutions.

**Africans:** This term was used for blacks, whereas non-whites meant Indians, coloureds and blacks.

**African School Compounds**: Established by various religious denominations working in Basutoland. These consisted of a Church, secondary or elementary boarding school, often a clinic, staff and church ministers.

**Afrikaans:** South African dialect developed from Dutch.

**Afrikaner:** A South African of Dutch descent.

**A K 47:** Abbreviation for "Assault Kalashnikov", the standard Eastern Bloc infantry weapon; it was popular with guerrilla movements worldwide.

**Amaqabane:** (pronounced — ama-ka-ba-nay) comrades, radical young and often undisciplined Township (Areas outside towns where blacks were allowed to live) Activists with loose ties to the UDF (United Democratic Front) and the ANC (African National Congress)

**assegai:** stabbing spear used by the Zulus.

**Azania:** Ancient Roman name for S-E Africa. ANC supporters rejected the name, claiming that it meant "place of slaves".

**baasskap:** In South Africa it meant the total domination of whites over blacks.

**Bantustan Area:** An area set aside by the white government for the exclusive occupation of African people. Also called "Homelands" since they were created around the tribal areas where they were born.

**Basutoland:** Region between the Orange and Caledon Rivers in which Moshoeshoe (pronounced mo-shoe-ay-shoe-ay) built up his Sotho Kingdom which became a British Protectorate in 1868. It gained its independence as Lesotho in 1966.

**Bechuanaland:** British Protectorate until 1966 when it became independent as Botswana.
**biltong:** jerked (cured in the sun) meat.

**black spot:** Land settled or owned by Africans and surrounded by or contiguous with predominantly "white" residential, industrial or agricultural areas. In terms of grand apartheid "black spots" must be eliminated.
**Boer:** South African of Dutch or Huguenot descent. It is from the Dutch for "farmer".
**Boers:** suffered from xenophobia. It was a dislike, hatred and fear of strangers or aliens.
**Bo-Mè:** The Ladies or The Women in Sesotho, language of the Basotho.
**Bophuthatswana:** Independent State created for the Tswana People. It included 7 pieces of disjointed areas in the Transvaal, Cape and Orange Free States of South Africa.
**BOSS:** (Bureau of State Security) Security police bureau established in 1969 by John Vorster and Hendrik van der Bergh. It was disbanded and replaced by the National Intelligence Service (1978), after Vorster's fall from grace.
**Broederbond:** Literally "Afrikaner" Brotherhood. An exclusively Afrikaner Society formed in 1918. It secured and maintained Afrikaner control in important areas such as government, culture, finance and industry.
**burgher:** Dutch term meaning citizen.
**bushveld:** Lowveld (fields) of north eastern Transvaal province
**Cambridge Overseas 0-Level Examinations:** Known as the Junior Certificate Course in Lesotho. Students wrote these external exams, administered by the University of Pretoria. These exams were equivalent to our Grade Ten. The higher certificate was the A-Levels.
**cattle:** Basutoland had a "pastoral economy" and a man's wealth was measured by the number of cattle that he possessed. They were used as the "bride-price". The groom had to pay so many head of cattle for his bride. The number was

often calculated by the education level that the girl had attained.

**coif:** Was the head covering made of gauze and linen that the religious women wore to distinguish the group to which they belonged. The one that Johnna wore was shaped like a "covered wagon" used in the old American West.

**coloured:** This described a person of mixed descent, usually a white with an African or Asian.

**colour bar:** Reservations of certain categories of work for persons of a particular race. The most menial jobs were given to blacks or Asians.

**compound:** Enclosures or living quarters in which the African mineworkers were housed, usually attached to a mine. They were not for families but for men only.

**Conservative Party (CP):** Ultra-right wing political party formed after the split in the NP in 1982 over adoption of the new constitution.

**Crossroads:** Squatter community on the Cape Flats south of Cape Town, occupied mainly by Coloureds.

**despotism:** A system of government in which the leader has unlimited power.

**dongas:** Large ditches caused by rain and/or wind erosion.

**a drift:** A ford over a stream or river.

**endorse out:** To endorse the reference book (Pass book) of an African, requiring him/her to leave a particular area and return to his "location" or "homeland".

**Front-line states:** Independent African States bordering or close to South Africa. These included Angola, Botswana, Lesotho, Malawi, Mozambique, Swaziland, Tanzania, Zambia and Zimbabwe.

**fundi:** A wise and knowledgeable person.

**gangsterism**: With gangsterism came vendettas, banditry, protection rackets, individual and group psychosis, competition for turf and treasures, a spreading mood of anarchy. What the Basotho called "Tsotsi-ism".

**great silence:** In religious communities at that time "great silence" started at 9 p.m. until after breakfast.

**gumbo:** A heavy, clayey soil that is sticky and non-porous when wet; thick clinging mud.

**Herrenvolk:** Master Race

**Highveld:** High altitude, summer rainfall grassland regions of the Transvaal, most of OFS, lying between 1200-1800 metres a.s.l.

**homeland:** Region where members of a particular African Language Group were offered self-government by the N.P. Ten ethnic areas of highly broken up areas were created but were never accepted as Independent by the rest of the world.

**ichiBemba:** Language of Zambia's northern Bemba Tribe

**Indaba(Zulu) and Puteho (Sotho):** A topic, being discussed at a general meeting of all the people; like a town meeting

**Influx control:** Regulations controlling the movement of Africans out of their Reserves or Homelands into "white" South Africa.

**internal colonialism:** Marxist concept used to describe political and economic inequalities between regions within a given society. Describes race inequalities for the underprivileged, the exploitation within a society.

**internecine struggles:** This involves struggles within a homogenous group; mutually destructive and usually fomented from without for political purposes.

**ISCOR:** Iron and Steel Industrial Corporation established as a public utility in 1927, in order to develop South Africa's own smelting industry.

**jambok:** a whip used against the blacks in South Africa.

**Job Reservation:** Regulations reserving certain jobs exclusively for workers of a particular group (white, Coloureds etc.) to enforce Grand Apartheid in the Western Cape, which became a "coloured preference" area, such as Crossroads.

**kaofela:** Sotho for everybody or all of them.

**Kaffir farming:** The letting of land to Africans thus creating pools of African labour on the Transvaal provinces' farms in the late 19th Century This pool was then made available to mine recruiting agencies for a large commission to the owner of the land.

**Kangaroo Court:** Unofficial courts set up by Township African activists to try those whom they saw as "offenders" for helping the "whites". They used tires around the neck which were set on fire as a form of punishment.

**Khoikhoi:** Literally means "men of men". They were herders who inhabited large areas of South Africa.

**Khoisan:** The collective name for the Khoikhoi (herders) and the San (hunters and gatherers).

**Khotso! Pula! Nala! Lehlohonolo!:** Peace! Rain! Abundance! Blessings! Upon meeting, the elder person starts the greetings by Pula and it is continued back and forth.

**kimberlite:** Type of rock in which diamonds may be found. Also called blue ground.

**kleurlingen:** Literally "Dutch and black mix."; Dutch term for people of colour.

**kloof:** mountain pass, gorge or ravine.

**knopkierie:** Afrikaans for knobkerrie, a type of stick used as a beating club.

**Koranto ea Becoana:** Bechuana Gazette established in 1901, until independence in 1966.

**kraal:** South African native village enclosed by a wall; also a pen to hold animals.

**kwela:** Literally "To jump up"; a musical style derived from the African rhythms and American swing, popularly played on a penny whistle. Kwela Jazz, a more sophisticated Kwela with the saxophone replacing the penny whistle.

**labyrinthine security:** Complicated network of security with censorship laws.

**Liberation Doctrine:** Methods and efforts by which oppressed people planned to achieve their liberation.

**lobolo:** Bride-wealth, money, property or services given by a prospective bridegroom to the father of his bride in order to establish his marital rights. In Basutoland it was as much as twelve head of cattle depending on the girl's education.

**A location:** A township for Africans usually situated near a "white" area.

**Lowveld:** low-lying areas east of the great escarpment in eastern Transvaal province.

**miscegenation:** Mixture of races; especially whites with a dark race.

**mixed marriage:** Not to be confused with the religious expression, it is a union between a white and black [African, or Coloured, or Indian] person. It was outlawed between 1949 and 1985.

**mud walls or huts:** These were made from a mixture of clay and cow dung which dried as cement. It was referred to as the "local cement".

**mynheer:** Afrikaans for mister. Also "meneer".

**Natives' Representative Council:** Established in 1936 after the last Africans were removed from the Cape voter's roll. It was abolished in 1951.

**Nkosi Sikelel' i Afrika:** God bless Africa, composed by Enoch Sontonga in 1862 and now the anthem of the ANC and part of the new anthem for South Africa.

**N U S A:** National Union of SA Students' Association. It consisted mainly of English speaking liberal student bodies and was founded in 1924.

**PASS:** A document which all Africans were required to carry on them to "prove" that they were "allowed" to enter or leave a "white" urban area. African's couldn't stay in white urban area more than 72 hours without a "pass".

**pellagra:** A disease caused by lack of food particularly a vitamin deficiency; lack of niacin, occurs in people whose staple diet is corn. Or it may be caused by the malabsorption of food caused by chronic diarrhea. Long standing pellagra can result in dementia and death.

**people's education:** Alternative to the "Bantu Education" forced on Africans in South Africa; not watered down thus preparing them to gain higher education in colleges and universities outside the country in a post-apartheid society.

**"petty" apartheid:** Enforced segregation of public amenities such as benches, beaches, buses, trains and toilets etc.

**pomponyane:** Referred to the accumulation of crusty material from sick, runny eyes. According to the Africans all blue eyes were sick or weak eyes.

**proletarian**: An industrial wage earner; a manual labourer.

**Rand:** Short for Witwatersrand, the gold bearing "Ridge of white waters" upon which Johannesburg is built. The Reef Another name for the Witwatersrand, derived from the vein of "reef" which is a lode of ore, in this case gold.

**Rand:** Principal unit of South African currency, greatly devalued after Independence.

**Reference book:** 96-page document carried by all Africans in "white" South Africa after 1952. It had to be carried at all times and produced on demand by the authorities. Specifically, it detailed the residence and pertinent information as well as working rights.

**R.C.M.:** Roman Catholic Mission. Each Mission had a resident priest and/or Sisters, an elementary school, sometimes a secondary school with boarding facilities and a clinic were also on sight. Apart from the Sisters it was the same set-up for other denominations.

**Taal:** Low Dutch language.

**Torch:** British term for flashlight

**Transition:** Referred to the transfer from formal Apartheid to informal stratification in 1992.

**sand fleas**: Because of the eight or nine months of drought and the sandy soils, Basutoland experiences sand fleas.

**SASO:** South African Students' Organization which was a black consciousness university movement formed in 1969 with Steve Biko as president.

**SASOL:** Parastatal industry established in 1950 to manufacture petroleum from coal.

**shebeen:** Where liquor was sold usually without a legal licence. Shabeens were common in the African townships.

**"school" Africans:** Western educated or mission educated Africans.

**segregation:** Policy of racial separation.

**Separate Development**: It was an attempt to glamorize apartheid by insisting that it fostered the development of each "racial" and language group.
**Southern Sotho**: Language spoken by Africans in the general area of Lesotho and the Orange Free State.
**Soweto:** An acronym for "South Western Township", a contiguous group of African townships south-west of Johannesburg.
**State of Emergency:** Suspension of certain civil liberties in order to strengthen the arm of the executive in controlling a perceived threat to the state.
**Swartegevaar**: Literally "black threat" or "black peril"; fear by white South Africans that they would be swamped by the African majority.
**subsistence farming:** Farming in which most of the produce is consumed by the farmer and his family, leaving little or none to be marketed.
**Transkei**: Area east of the Kei River, settled by the Xhosa chiefdoms and administered as a district of the Cape Province. It became a Bantustan and was granted sell-government in 1963 and Independence in 1976. It was not accepted by the international Community as valid.
**Treason Trial:** Of the 156 ANC members and others following the civil disobedience campaign of the early 1950's.
**veld:** Grasslands with scattered shrubs and small trees. From the Dutch for field.
**Verglites:** Afrikaners
**VW Kombi:** Volkswagon minibus was the common mode of transport in the missions in the 1960's.
**Uitlander:** Alien, foreigner particularly said of a Briton living in South Africa in the 1890's.
**UDF:** United Democratic Front established in 1983.
**ubuntu**: (I am because we are). Zulu word meaning humaness. The concept of ubuntu an African philosophy and way of life. Hindus call it SoHum (That is I and I am that).
**Umkhonto we Sizwe:** Literally "the spear of the nation", military wing of the ANC. It was established soon after the organization was banned in the 1960s.

**ululations:** A howling or wailing used by the African women to express communal emotions, such as joy or war, etc.

**verkrampte:** Said of a close-minded conservative South African Boer.

**volk:** People or nation in Afrikaans.